MW01275741

My other books:
Shelter from Thunder
Shades of Grey
Underneath
Bits of Cargill
Jake
Saying Goodbye to Warsaw

Email - mcargill79@gmail.com
Twitter - @MichaelCargill1
Website of satire -
http://michaelcargill.wordpress.com/
http://www.facebook.com/MichaelCargillAuthor

My thanks go to the group moderators on
Goodreads and to everyone who assisted me during
the editing process.

Chapter One

Somewhere in Normandy, about a month after the D-Day landings in July of 1944.

"The thing that you Dunkirk veterans don't seem to realise," Captain Jones began explaining to the rest of his squad, "is that you're not actually veterans of anything at all; all you did was run away when the going got tough."

As James cast a frown at his commanding officer, the low sound of muttering and grumbling drowned out the soft whisper of his boots moving through the grass.

"Us lot who served in North Africa though?" Jones continued, pressing a thumb against his chest just to make sure that everyone knew who he was referring to, "We fought our way across the baking desert and tickled the balls of Mr Nazi bigwig Field Marshall Rommel himself. And it's the likes of me who'll be winning this war."

As if to demonstrate just how expansive his experience was, Jones took an exaggerated step over a dried cow pat. "Mind the shit, yeah?" he advised those behind him.

"Anyone know why they nicknamed us the Desert Rats?" he continued, speaking in a lofty tone that suggested he wasn't actually expecting any of them to provide an answer.

"Was it because you're annoying and no-one liked you?" someone quietly quipped from the back.

Jones turned his head and quickly scanned the group of seven soldiers under his command but was unable to see who had dared to interrupt him. "It's because we were small and fierce," he explained, "and no matter how many times Rommel thought he had us trapped in a corner, we fought back and won."

"The British Army is lucky to have you, Sir," a soldier cheerily remarked with a hint of sarcasm.

"Too bloody right they are," Jones agreed without a hint of irony, "you ain't gonna win any wars by running away and I didn't do no running away."

A pang of annoyance ran through James and he noisily cleared his throat as he readied himself to voice some kind of protest. Although the inglorious retreat back through France to the coast of Dunkirk was four years in the past, the memories of it were still fresh and vivid in his mind and he didn't appreciate being mocked for events that were well beyond his control.

"Got something to say, Corporal?" Jones challenged him.

"Well, Sir," James began, "it's just that the war isn't over yet."

"Congratulations on figuring that out. It's good to see that you Dunkirkians are still learning on the job."

"What I meant was that the war in Africa is over and you Desert Rats ran away at least twice before you finally won. But the war for us Dunkirk veterans is still going. You might have tickled Rommel's private parts, but we're going to march into Berlin and pull Hitler's pants down. And then we'll roast his balls on an open fire and feed them to him."

Jones glared at him as his mind scraped around for some kind of a comeback until James shrugged and found something on the horizon to focus on. In the silence that followed he received nods and smiles from those around him whilst David, who James was most familiar with, took a final drag from his cigarette and theatrically flicked it over James' head, sending sparks of burning tobacco shooting off in all directions. The opportunity for further jovialities was squashed when the drone of an approaching airplane quickly had eight pairs of eyes nervously scanning the sky in search of the tell-tale black speck.

"Okay, everyone get down!" Jones barked.

Not for the first time, James noted how quickly things could change from one moment to the next. One minute you could be having a pointless argument with a superior officer and a mere heartbeat later everyone is diving for cover. It was as if the world were a giant school playground and behind every corner lay a bully that was waiting to smash you to pieces. A black shape popped out from behind a cloud and flew right above their heads. On the underside of the wings James could make out the black and white cross of the Luftwaffe, a sight that filled him with a sense of awe and fear. Although the power of these flying machines was impressive on its own, the infamous symbols associated with German military might seemed to possess a supernatural deadliness of their own, one that dusted and sowed fear wherever it went. As the plane disappeared from view the soldiers relaxed and stood back up again.

"I think that's the same plane we've been seeing for the past couple of days," one of the soldiers

3

remarked, peering through the scope of his sniper rifle.

"Don't be daft, you're just paranoid," scoffed Jones.

"No, he's right," corrected James, "it's the same type and I recognised the faded Swastika on its tail."

"What do you mean it was the same type? All those Nazi planes are the same."

"Nah, they ain't. You've got the Stuka bombers, the Messerschmitt, the Heinkel, the -"

Jones interrupted him and waved his hand dismissively. "Alright, Professor, enough showing off. We've only got another hour of daylight left so let's get moving again."

The sniper waved his rifle in James' direction. "Pipe don't lie to me, what she sees is the truth."

David scrunched his face up. "You what?"

"Pipe," the sniper repeated, tenderly patting his favoured weapon. "My trusty Pipe has been with me through thick and thin ever since I signed up in thirty-eight. This scope is her eye and we've done plenty of sightseeing together."

There was a moment of silence as the rest of them tried to make sense of what they were hearing.

"Do you take her to bed with you?" one of them asked.

A jovial grin appeared on the sniper's face. "What sort of man doesn't like a bit of female company at night?"

"I'm glad I didn't share barracks with you," someone replied, sending a low ripple of laughter through the group.

"Do you clean it every day?" asked James, "It's in good condition for something that's about six years old."

"Nah," the sniper answered with a twinkle in his eye, "she jammed herself after six months so I had to get the barrel replaced. Then I dropped her out the window during training and smashed the scope to pieces. In fact, I accidentally left her on the train a fortnight before D-Day and lost her forever. Got myself a newer model though, so it weren't all bad."

There was more laughter and it was louder this time.

"But she's still me trusty old Pipe. Pipe's spirit will always be with me, God bless her soul."

"You're like the Pied Piper of bloody Hamelin," David remarked, a freshly lit cigarette hanging from his mouth.

Piper's wide grin exposed a missing tooth. "I like that and I think Pipe likes it, too. I do believe that you're quite the ladies' man, Dave."

David coughed in surprise, an involuntary reaction that sent the cigarette tumbling from his mouth and caused him to burn his fingers as he flailed around trying to catch it again. He scowled in annoyance, shoved it back between his lips, and didn't look back at Piper. Once the laughter had died down, James noted with regret how brief these periods of amusement could be. The days were filled with a potent mixture of boredom and danger, with laughter only ever existing as a thin coat of icing and he wondered how long it would be before the next playground bully showed up. Twenty minutes later Captain Jones decided that the day was more or less over and they started to make camp under some trees. Trench tools were unpacked and the air was soon filled with the sound of metal spades being thrust into the ground to turn over the soft French soil. James finished digging his own foxhole just as the sun was going down and he lay on his back to marvel at the burning sunset.

"Red sky at night, soldier's delight," he murmured, mostly to himself.

Piper rolled over and faced him. "Melancholy evening, German wife is grieving," he remarked with a grin.

James shot him a weak smile but remained silent, content to just lie there idly listening to the snippets of conversation that rose up every now and then. Shortly before the world descended into darkness, David came over and sat down next to him. James knew how rare it was to see a genuine smile appear on David's face - it was an event that only took place if he needed something or if he thought he had found something that was going to make him rich.

"Don't suppose you got any spare smokes on you?" David enquired conversationally.

James dug two cigarettes out from his pocket and handed them over. Although he didn't actually smoke himself, James still made sure he received the ration that he was entitled to; they were pretty much a form of currency and were considered legal tender by nearly everyone he bumped into these days. Whether a person was French, American, Australian, or even German, the one thing that was guaranteed to get the wheels greased was tobacco.

"Moon is looking big tonight," James remarked.

6

David looked across at James with a frown. As far as he was concerned the moon was the moon no matter what country it was looking down at him from. "Yup," he agreed noncommittally after a moment of silence.

James grinned to himself in the darkness. During all his time as a soldier, one of the only constants of his job was the eventual appearance of the moon at night. No matter how far he had to march and no matter how warm or cold it was, that bright round object was always there in the sky when the day was over.

"I'm going to grab some sleep," David said, letting out a yawn.

James listened as David's boots stumbled and clumped their way back to his hole when a series of bright flashes suddenly appeared on the horizon. From this distance the boom of artillery guns was as faint and as harmless as the sound of a newspaper dropping through a letterbox but the lightshow was fascinating and hypnotic to watch. Although he knew that the people back home in Britain would find it hard to understand, James was more than willing to admit that war was capable of producing wonderful moments of spectacular beauty. After the shelling had eventually stopped, James looked back up at the moon and wondered which war was responsible for its pitted, ravaged surface.

From his inside pocket he fished out a photograph and gazed at it fondly. Although it was far too dark for him to actually see anything, James didn't need any light to get comfort from the face of Mary, the beloved girl who was patiently waiting for him back home, and he used his finger to trace round the edges of her face and across her soft lips. Although she looked beautiful in the photo it was nothing more than a snapshot of her, a mere copy that was no closer to the real thing than a quick sketch would be. James remembered the morning when the postman had delivered the brown envelope to their house: Mary had anxiously ummed and ahhed over the photos, unable to decide which one she liked best or whether she even liked any of them at all. He kissed her on the cheek and explained that no mere cameraman could ever capture the full range of her beauty on film, that no photographer could ever imprint her intelligence, her wit, or her charm onto a flimsy bit of card. She had smiled at him then, her face taking on that girlish look that reminded him that no matter how strong and independent she seemed to be on the outside, underneath lay a vulnerable person who still needed reassurance every now and then.

He thought back to how he had first met her in a pub, some six months after his return from Dunkirk. Across the other side of the room he caught sight of two girls sitting themselves down at a table, glasses of wine balanced expertly in their hands. At first James thought that she was just another pretty face in the crowd but after a while he found himself drawn to the way she smiled and gestured with her hands as she spoke. Even the smoke from her cigarette seemed to hover and linger as if it were reluctant to go elsewhere. She glanced over at him a number of times, holding his gaze for a second or two until another patron walked across her line of sight. He sat there pondering whether it was worth going over and chatting to her, weighing up the possibility that she was either already engaged to someone or was merely visiting the area. As the minutes ticked by he was finally spurred him into action when he realised that he wasn't the only man who had taken a fancy to her.

The perfect opportunity to introduce himself arose when her friend stood up and disappeared in the direction of the toilet. In his eagerness to act before anyone else, James accidentally banged his leg against the table, sending the empty ashtray sliding loudly across the smooth polished surface. Although he made a grab for it he was too slow and it hit the thinly carpeted floor with an audible *thunk* that was impossible for anyone to have missed. After picking it up and tossing it back onto the table he looked over at the girl and, although she wasn't actually looking in his direction, there seemed to be a ghost of a smile on her lips that suggested she had seen everything. James took a deep breath, swallowed his pride, and made his way over to her.

"Hello," he said, suddenly aware that he wasn't sure what to say next.

She looked up at him and smiled coyly. "Hello," she replied.

"Do you come here often?"

She gave a small shrug and the haze of cigarette smoke seemed to move with the bob of her head. "I've been here once or twice, I think. How about you?"

"I've been here plenty of times. I only live down the road."

She nodded in agreement and the coy smile reappeared, leading James to think that she was just teasing him for her own amusement. "Tell me, that newspaper I saw you reading over on that table," she began, pointing past him, "I didn't see you turning any pages; you're either a slow reader or you were distracted by something far more interesting than the headlines."

James glanced over at where he had been sitting, suddenly aware that he hadn't been as discreet with his admiring stares as he thought he had been. He looked back at the girl and saw that she was now looking directly into his eyes, almost as if she was challenging him to prove his mettle. James stared at her for a moment, watching as the cigarette smoke swirled protectively in front of her face as if it had decided that he shouldn't be anywhere near her, thinking that this girl was far too self-assured, far too confident for him to handle. He glanced down at her ashtray and smiled as he realised something.

"That cigarette there in front of you," he said, gesturing down at the table, "there's no lipstick on it so it's been nowhere near your mouth. Perhaps you were distracted by something more interesting...?"

The girl's eyes involuntarily flicked down and then back up again, her lips parting in momentary shock. She tried to hold his gaze again but her cockiness was broken and she let out a small girlish giggle that made her sound surprisingly vulnerable.

"Okay, you got me there," she confessed, "I don't actually smoke but I like to use them as a little prop sometimes."

James smiled back at her and held his hand out. "My name's James, it was a pleasure to be distracted by you."

She laughed and took his hand. "I'm Mary. Grab your newspaper and maybe we can do the crossword together."

James retrieved the paper and sat down at her table. A few minutes later, Mary's friend returned and the three of them spent the best part of an hour working their way through the clues. After buying the three of them some drinks, James was pleasantly surprised when the two girls insisted on paying for the subsequent rounds afterwards. It turned out that the pair of them worked in the Auxiliary Territorial Service, the women's branch of the British Army, and damn proud of it they were too.

"My gun's bigger than yours" Mary teased him as they explained their work with the anti-aircraft guns.

The trio ended up staying in the pub for far longer and ended up considerably merrier than any of them had originally planned to be.

"We only popped in for a quick one," Mary admitted, "but I've always said that the unplanned nights out are the best ones."

After the landlord finally managed to convince them that it was time to go home, James escorted the two women to their bus stop and received a kiss on the cheek from each of them. Mary wrote her address and phone number down on a piece of paper and expressed her desire to meet up with him again.

"If you don't call me or come knocking for me," she told him, "I'll be forced to track you down and demand an explanation as to why not."

Her friend cackled loudly and warned James that she wasn't joking.

Over the course of the next three weeks the two of them met up as often as their respective jobs allowed them to and although neither confessed to it at the time, they had to do a considerable amount of juggling and swapping around of their shifts with colleagues in order to make time for each other. One particular evening, as they walked along the riverfront and bought themselves a bag of hot chips each, James watched in baffled silence as Mary proceeded to drown hers in vinegar.

"I love my chips all soggy and sour," she explained with a giggle, "also means no-one else will try to pinch them when I'm not looking."

As they slowly made their way along the path, Mary seemed more interested in feeding the local ducks than herself until one particular bird squawked noisily at her.

"Don't you quack at me, Mr Swan," she called back across the water, "if you don't like vinegar you should bloody well say so."

James laughed and felt a sudden compulsion to pull her towards him. He found himself delighted by her brightness and drawn towards her mannerisms, whilst her flirtatiousness never failed to send a thrill running through him. As a result of sharing most of her dinner with the local wildlife Mary finished her chips well before James did. She leaned in and grabbed herself a small handful from his bag, only to grimace when she popped them into her mouth.

"Yuck! You've drenched them in salt you fiend, what's wrong with you?"

James laughed once again and this time he *did* pull her towards him, kissing her full on the mouth.

They remained together for a few seconds until she pulled back, causing the squashed remains of James' takeaway dinner to fall to the floor. Mary blinked up at him and James wondered if he had blown his chances entirely.

"You're very bold, James," she playfully scolded him, "but I like bold as much as I like handsome."

Although she was trying to act cool, James could see that her face was flushed red and the rise and fall of her chest betrayed just how breathless she was.

"Kiss me again," she demanded, a wish that was duly granted.

James eased the photo back into his pocket and settled himself down into his foxhole. The stench of fresh mud served only to remind him just how far away from home he was and when he looked up at the moon one last time, he hoped that Mary was doing the same thing.

***

Chapter Two

James was awoken the next morning by quite possibly the loudest belch he had ever heard.

"Wake you up did I?" enquired Piper with a grin.

James grunted with displeasure and lifted himself out from his cramped sleeping quarters. The sky was bright and the comforting presence of the moon had been replaced by the scattered uncertainty of ruffled clouds rolling from one end of the horizon to the other. A thin column of smoke could be seen rising from the direction of the shelling that he had been watching only a few hours ago.

"Reckon that's us or them?" Piper asked.

James paused before answering, not entirely sure if Piper was referring to which side had done the shelling or which side was now licking its wounds. "Them," he answered, before clarifying it with, "I reckon we've given Jerry another smashing."

Piper nodded in agreement and stared out across the French countryside. "Jerry, Jerry, quite contrary. How does your garden grow?"

"With silver bells, and cockle shells, and pretty maids all in a row," finished James and the two of them grinned at each other.

"Have you two ladies finished?" the captain enquired sarcastically, "Get your stuff packed up so we can get going."

There was muttering and noise as the eight men urinated and collected their gear together. Empty cigarette packets were kicked and tossed into the vacated holes that they would soon be abandoning forever, leaving James to wonder just how much of the French countryside would be pockmarked like this by the time the war was over. The group finally set off again, with the silence punctuated only by the occasional bit of idle chatter and the clunking of equipment. To stave off the boredom James kept an eye on the horizon for either the return of the German plane or signs of more artillery fire whilst David hung near the back, happy to just smoke cigarettes and let the others do the thinking for now.

"Sir, why don't you tell us a story about your time in North Africa?" someone loudly suggested.

Captain Jones raised his head up from the map he had been studying. "Why? It was hot, humid, and too dangerous for you lot; that's all you need to know."

There was a moment of silence before someone else spoke up. "Yeah, but I saw a film at the cinema where you lot were frying eggs on the side of the tanks. It might've been hot but it can't be that dangerous if you've got time for an egg and bacon butty."

Piper looked round at James and grinned, who grinned back at him.

"I faced more tanks and guns out there than any of you boys will ever see," Jones responded, "we covered half the desert in landmines and blew up every building that didn't belong to us."

"Yeah, but these eggs. Were they shipped over or were they laid by local chickens? 'Cos I reckon if a chicken could survive out there, it couldn't have been too scary." A number of sniggers rippled across the group.

"Private?" Jones began, "Be quiet."

Throughout this exchange David had remained silent but attentive. He didn't have much time for the captain's boasts, especially when he hadn't seen any sign that Jones was the great warrior he seemed to think he was, but he was becoming concerned that he was being led by a loud incompetent who was going to get him killed.

"We should have reached this town by now," muttered Jones.

"What're we going there for anyway, Sir?" one of them asked.

"We're like an advance party, got to get there and hold tight until we receive further orders."

David frowned. Why would a veteran of North Africa be sent on such a meaningless mission? And why were they walking rather than being driven? He turned around to look at James, who just shrugged and rolled his eyes. They soon came upon a lone tractor that looked as if it had been abandoned. Although it wasn't a vehicle that usually elicited much excitement, to men who've been walking for two days straight it was a tantalising sight.

"Let's drive the rest of the way there," David urged, "no-one else is using it."

"It still belongs to someone, Private," Jones condescendingly reminded him.

David wasn't in the least bit interested in such details. As far as he was concerned, if someone leaves a tractor right in the middle of nowhere when there is a war on, they lose their right to complain if it gets taken. "So? Save us walking so far."

"It might be booby trapped," warned James, "the moment you turn that ignition, you'll set off a grenade or there'll be a mine buried just in front of the wheels."

David looked back at the vehicle, something that a few moments ago was a glorious prize but was now nothing more than a poisoned chalice.

"Hey, is that the top of a church?" one of them asked, pointing at something in the distance.

Piper raised his rifle and peered through the scope. "It sure is," he confirmed.

"Does it look friendly?" enquired Jones, a question that generated a few quizzical looks. "I mean, does it look like they're worshipping at the altar of the Nazi almighty?" he testily added.

"Dunno," shrugged Piper, "if they do, they certainly haven't lugged it out and put it up on the roof."

"Right, well everyone keep an eye out anyway. Don't want to go blundering into the local German headquarters."

Half an hour later they closed in on what looked to be a small town. Piper periodically squinted through his scope but couldn't see any signs of military occupation. They walked past a battered wooden sign that looked as if it had been attacked by a hammer, with the word *pique* just about visible on it.

"Smith!" the Captain barked at a volume that left James to assume that the notion of approaching quietly and covertly had been abandoned, "You speak French. How'd you pronounce that?"

"You pronounce it like 'peek' but it looks like we're only seeing half of the sign. And my name's Smythe, Sir"

The captain rolled his eyes. "Smith, Smythe. Tomato, potato. Chinese, Japanese."

As the group entered the outskirts of the town the hard smooth road felt strange and alien after days of marching across uneven countryside, and their heavy boots were loud and jarring as the houses threw the sound of their footsteps back at them. It seemed that the war was yet to touch this part of France to any great degree as most of the buildings were still intact, with only the occasional half-collapsed house betraying that not everything was right with the world. One house in particular looked as if it had been sliced in half with a giant knife, the inside rooms exposed and open like it was a child's dollhouse. They made their way through the streets, their progress opposed only by the occasional twitching curtain and gawping face that gaped at them as if they were a herd of naked savages. Word of their arrival seemed to spread and it wasn't long before people were coming out of their houses to stare at them. A crowd started following them in a way that caused the eight soldiers to feel peculiarly nervous and they drew ever closer together as the strange French chatter quickly increased in volume and intensity. James nodded and smiled at those nearest to him, an action that finally broke the deadlock. A pretty blonde girl of around nineteen ran up to him and threw her arms around his neck, covering his face with kisses.

"Handsome soldier! I love handsome British soldier!" she cried.

After more than a month spent in the confines of military barracks and sleeping outdoors, the smell of the girl's perfume and the sound of her exotic accent sent James' pulse racing. He gripped her hard, relishing the softness of her cheek against his unshaven face and the pressure of her breasts against his chest. She kissed him a final time on the lips before disappearing back into the crowd, leaving James to stare and lust after her as he realised just how much he was missing civilian home life. He glanced around at his fellow soldiers and saw that their pockets were being filled with gifts of food and drink. Brown bottles of beer were being thrust into Piper's hands, whilst the sudden influx of packets of tobacco and cigarettes explained the uncharacteristic smile spreading across David's face. Exclamations of delight in French and broken English filled the air, reminding James of the scenes of celebrations he had witnessed back in 1939. Back then, when the war had barely even started, the arrival of the British Expeditionary Force in Calais had been greeted by hordes of cheering French civilians, something which now seemed to have happened a lifetime ago. For perhaps the first time, James got an inkling of how much his life had changed since his first taste of military life.

Britannique! Americain! Anglais! We are saved! Churchill! Roosevelt!

James could hear Smythe shouting out phrases in French but he was fighting a losing battle to be heard above the din. Piper was now holding a bewildered-looking toddler in his arms, something that seemed to please him immensely as he tickled the young boy's belly, causing him to squeal in delight. James looked at Piper's face and thought he looked like a man who had just returned home to his family after a long trip away. He placed the child, who now seemed to have realised that a street party was in full swing, up onto his shoulders so that he could bounce around at the top of the world.

"Hey Cap, can we let this little one join our squad?" Piper asked, looking around for Jones, "he's a right friendly -"

The sound of a gunshot cut right through everything, causing the large crowd of French civilians to flinch and fall instantly silent. The sound of a child bursting into tears broke the silence and every smile seemed to vanish from the face of the earth.

"Alright, party is over," announced Jones as he slid his pistol back into the holster.

Piper shot him a furious look and lowered the trembling child gingerly back down to the ground. Smythe muttered a few apologetic French words to those around him before making one final quip with an exaggerated shrug and a roll of his eyes, sending a ripple of laughter through the crowd. Although James didn't speak French he had caught the word *capitaine* well enough and allowed himself a smile.

"Come on, we need to find the mayor or whoever is charge around here," Jones said, beckoning for everyone to follow him.

They soon came upon a grassy area that looked as if it served as a village green.

"Right, you lot stay here while I go and find some important people," instructed the captain, "Hopefully they can put us up somewhere."

The seven soldiers gladly slumped down and relaxed in the sunshine as they began sharing out their gifts. Hunks of cheese and meat were passed round so that everyone had a chance to gorge on something other than standard army rations, and bottles of beer and wine were uncapped and uncorked and swigged down, allowing Piper to let rip with a tremendous belch for the second time that day. James noted without surprise that David didn't bother to offer round any of the tobacco he had been given. A few minutes into the small party some shouting could be heard from across the road and James looked up to see an elderly woman shaking her fist at them from an open window. A number of passersby seemed to be shooing her to be quiet.

"Smythe, any idea what she's saying?" asked Piper.

Smythe turned his ear towards her and scrunched up his face as he strained to hear what the woman was saying. "Something about... I think she's angry at us 'cos her husband was a soldier in the last war. Seems he was shot by the British. Can't really make out the rest."

"Tell her that if he got shot by his own side, it was his probably his own stupid fault," David growled.

Although David received a few frowns for this outburst, Smythe duly went ahead and said something to her. A look of shock and outrage appeared on the woman's face and she slammed the window shut again.

"You didn't really tell her that did you?" asked James.

Smythe smiled. "Nah. Told her that David here was in love with her and was going to propose when the war was over."

A burst of laughter rang out from everyone else whilst David sat there in silence.

"Looks like you're not the ladies' man after all, eh, Dave?" Piper joked, exposing his missing tooth with another big grin. "Seems James is the one that the girls like today. That French blonde was all over him."

James smiled awkwardly and gave a small shrug. During his time as a soldier he had done many things that he didn't think a civilised person was capable of, most of which he could quite easily rationalise as a result of having to do whatever was needed to survive in the field of combat. However, one thing that he hadn't ever thought would be tested was his relationship with Mary and the willingness with which he had welcomed the advances of that girl surprised him.

Half an hour later, their captain returned just as some of them were beginning to doze off. "Smith, you should've come with me. Seems half the people in this place don't speak proper English."

"Sorry, Sir, but you didn't ask so -"

"Don't matter," said Jones, cutting him off, "there's an old building on the other side of town we can use for now. All of you, grab your stuff and follow me."

As they all got back to their feet, one or two of them winced as their stomachs battled against the rich cheese and wine they had consumed. David was expressionless as he lit himself another cigarette and double-checked that his tobacco was secure.

"The Germans were here up until about two weeks ago," Jones told them as they made their way along the road, "so don't be surprised if some of the folk here are a bit twitchy and jumpy. When they left, they took about two dozen civilians with them."

They all looked at the captain with interest. "What for?" asked Piper.

"Who knows," Jones answered with a shrug, "slave labour for their war factories perhaps, or maybe just because they're a bunch of Nazi bastards."

Ten minutes later they stopped outside an empty two-storey building. Although the roof was sagging and there were large cracks running down the front, it looked relatively intact and secure.

"I guess this is the place," Jones decided, pushing open the door.

A stench of staleness caused James to cough as he stepped inside and the dust that coated every surface left him wondering if it was safe to touch anything, but from what he could see the place was dry and free of any local wildlife.

"Oh, forgot to mention before," began Jones, "the mayor said that a German plane shows up every so often to shoot at the rooftops and anyone who has the misfortune to be outside. So keep an eye out for it."

James and Piper exchanged a glance as they wondered if it was the same plane that they had been seeing over the past couple of days.

"Well, find a space and make yourselves at home," the captain instructed them.

The building was split up into three rooms on the ground floor and four more upstairs that included a bathroom; much to their joy and surprise the water was working. David was the first to notice that one of the rooms had a fireplace and he quickly claimed himself a spot in the corner. James and Piper joined him, with everyone else making their own arrangements.

"Nice and cosy in here," quipped Piper as he cleared himself a space on the floor.

Although James agreed with Piper's assessment, David felt that if the townspeople were truly grateful that their country was being liberated they should have been prepared to offer up a nicer place to stay than this run-down shed that nobody else wanted. No doubt when the Nazis had first arrived they would have claimed the nicest houses for themselves and shot anyone who dared to disagree. Sitting beside the fireplace was a metal box and the hinges squealed in protest as he opened the lid.

"Well, they were nice enough to leave us a bit of coal and wood for the fire," David remarked, referring to both the Germans and the French.

James and Piper spent some time cleaning out the room to make it more hospitable, whilst David lit himself another cigarette and cleared out the fireplace. Once he was settled in James decided to do some exploring and after navigating his way round to the back of the building he found a small pile of rotting logs and a large rusty axe that looked as old and abandoned as the building it was leaning against. A small handcart that looked as if it had been used to transport wood was half-buried under a heap of dirt and leaves, and James let out a grunt as he struggled to pull it free. The wheels creaked and groaned as they fought against the rust and grime that was conspiring to weld them together, when a small rodent shot out and scurried away at such a speed that James wondered if he had simply seen a puff of smoke. He made his way through the grass and followed a faint path towards some trees and began to wonder if bringing the cart had been such a good idea after all – its constant clanking was more than loud enough to alert any nearby German patrols of his presence.

About a minute later he reached the edge of the woods and stopped as a bird noisily took wing and flew off in the direction of the town he had just come from. After watching it disappear over the rooftops he continued his journey again, old twigs and leaves crunching and snapping beneath his heavy boots. After collecting up some branches and small logs, he stopped for a rest on an old tree stump and pulled out a cigarette. Despite his distaste for smoking, he found the smell of tobacco strangely tantalising and he slid it back and forth across his top lip. After spending so much time in a state where he had to be ready to be called into action at any time, James found it strange to be sitting here in the woods all by himself - it was probably the first bit of peace and quiet he had had since arriving in France. He glanced around at the peaceful scenery, listening to the occasional tweeting of birds and the soft breeze passing through the trees. Out the corner of his eye he caught sight of something small and brown, yet when he turned his head there was nothing but a bobbing branch; presumably the wildlife was as distrusting and wary of his presence as it was curious. James looked back at the cart he had brought with him, the rust and decay looking out of place amongst this place of calm beauty. He breathed in sharply as its ugliness reminded him of the scenes on the beaches of Normandy.

Although the journey across the English Channel had been a noisy and tense affair, it had also been mercifully uneventful as thousands of men sailed across the sea in a hundred transport ships. As his world slowly rocked and rolled with the waves, James tried to avoid thinking about what would happen if they were hit by a torpedo or blundered into a mine, aware that the cramped conditions meant that his chances of survival were slim at best. When the shrill high-pitched sound of a dozen sentries blowing on their whistles cut through the air, a knot of sickness took hold in his belly as he realised that his role in the war was once again being called upon in earnest. Despite the sheer number of men making their way down to the loading bays very few people seemed to be talking, allowing the clunk of boots on the stairs and clank of equipment to dominate everything. As he stepped onto the landing craft that was going to take him and over a dozen other soldiers to the shore, he could feel the sea moving and shifting uneasily under his feet, and over the roar of the diesel engines he thought he heard someone wish him luck.

A minute later the craft surged forward and began zipping and bouncing its way over the waves towards French soil. The stench of the sea was broken by the occasional whiff of excrement as men

26

soiled themselves as they finally came to terms with what they were about to be undertaking. With the craft rising and falling with the waves, James snatched occasional glimpses of the beach and it was like no other coastline he had ever seen before. The huge expanse of sand was utterly devoid of sunbathers and holiday makers, instead filled with hundreds, probably *thousands,* of spikes and obstacles blocking the path of any uninvited tanks and armoured vehicles. The smell of vomit hung thick in the air as men emptied their stomachs, no doubt trying to convince themselves that they were merely seasick rather than utterly terrified.

James looked up at the sky and found it to be filled with immense flocks of seagulls floating and cawing high above him, no doubt curious about the overnight appearance of this gigantic armada that had appeared in their back garden. The familiar *whoosh* of an artillery shell caused him to duck instinctively before a large column of water washed over the side soaking him to the bone, giving him the excuse that his legs were shaking from the cold rather than because he thought he was about to die. He got one last look at the beach and all those spikes and obstacles had grown in size and number, when the craft shuddered and came to a halt as it met solid ground. Someone blew a whistle and a strange rattling vibration shuddered through the entire craft as the front ramp slammed down into the water.

The world had turned mad.

The moment James stepped forward he knew that something was wrong. The men in front of him seemed to be tripping and stumbling as if someone had tied their shoelaces together for a joke, and the air was filled with a warm red mist that kept springing up from nowhere. He stepped over someone, finding himself annoyed that a soldier would choose that place in particular to lie down, when to his horror he saw that one half of the man's head was missing. To his left there was a sudden roar as a section of the beach leapt into the air and towered over him like a gigantic phoenix rising up from the earth. Some men ran past him and he followed them in a bewildered daze, hoping that they knew where they were going, when one of them fell over and didn't get back up again. For reasons he couldn't quite grasp the ground was covered with lumps of flesh and a dark redness, with guns and crates of equipment left lying around where anyone might trip over them. He spotted a crater in the sand and threw himself into it, landing next to a soldier wearing an unusual uniform, his face pale and full of terror.

"They're *everywhere!*" the soldier screamed in a shrill American accent, "these cocksucking mother -" before slumping down and never saying another word again.

James blinked as his mind flailed and grasped to get a hold on the reality of what was going on around him, with men cowering behind metal tank obstacles as they screamed and wailed for their mothers. The ground was littered with soldiers who were either dead or dying, the air filled with the panic-stricken shrieks and wails of fully grown men regressing to the mental state of naked and defenceless infants. The whoosh of incoming artillery shells was unending and the roar of explosions, throwing up entire sections of the beach and tossing people aside as if they were made of paper, was overwhelming. Further up the beach lay nothing but cliffs and immense concrete bunkers that rose into the air like monoliths, the machine gun fire as relentless as a thousand alarm clocks going off at once. Every so often James was aware of something zipping past his head, something so tiny that it couldn't been seen, yet so hot and deadly that it could easily smash his head to smithereens if it wanted to, almost as if the propeller of a low flying Spitfire had missed him by a mere inch.

He watched helplessly as men who had spent five years training for this moment were obliterated before his eyes, dissolving into red mists as if they were nothing more than cigarette ash in the wind. A paralysing fear began to grip him as his senses were overloaded with the sheer noise and chaos going on around him. It was as though every single choir boy was singing every single word of every single song that had ever been written and he was being forced to listen to all of them at once. His fingers wormed themselves into the cold French sand as the panic rose up through his chest to envelop him and he was powerless to run away from it. Another soldier suddenly slumped down next to him, his elbow catching James in the head, momentarily stunning him and breaking him out of his trance. An absurd fury surged through him as he remembered how much he hated it when people tried to push and barge their way past him. James clenched his hand into a fist and slammed it into the man's helmet, not caring who he was or whose side he was on.

"What are you doing, you stupid bastard?" he screamed, "Get up! Get out of my face and start moving!"

The soldier looked round at James, his eyes full of fear and horror, something that sent James into an apoplectic rage. What use was all the training and equipment if everyone was going to sit and cower inside the first hole they found? He stood up and began bellowing at everyone around him to move, to get off their backsides, to get up the beach and do something. Although most of them stared at him like petrified rabbits, a few listened to him and James didn't care if it was out of fear or honour: he just wanted them to move. As he passed other groups of cowering soldiers, his face boiled red with rage and his throat burned as he hounded and harried his followers up the beach, the group swelling in size as men gravitated towards him; before he knew it they were all standing in front of a bare cliff face with nowhere else to go. He looked up at the sheer impenetrable wall helplessly, realising that he had led them all into a death-trap… yet they were all looking at him, a mere corporal, their eyes begging him to tell them what to do. His foot banged against something and when he looked down he saw that all manner of crates had been carried up the beach with them.

"What's all this shit?" he demanded, wondering if he had unwittingly assembled a company of porters and servants.

"Explosives!" someone yelled back in an Australian accent.

James blinked as the germ of an idea took hold somewhere in his mind. "We got any engineers here?"

A cacophony of shouts and hands went up, something that briefly sent James into a state of euphoria. "Can we blow this cliff up?"

"That an order or a question?" the Australian asked, without bothering to wait for an answer.

Close to a dozen men sprang into action, breaking open the crates and dragging the contents over to a section in the cliff. Moments later the sound of pick axes, bayonets, and spades chipping away at the rock filled the air, attracting the attention of several German soldiers high above them. Bullets started raining down on them but this time everyone was psyched up and ready and willing to return fire in earnest. Every so often a *bling!* sound filled the air as the Americans ejected the empty clips from their rifles, a sound that mixed in with the steady *tick tick tick* from the engineers to create an absurd percussion instrument concert. Although the wait for the explosives team to finish their work was agonising, James was now infused with a sense of purpose that kept him going as he bellowed out shouts and commands every time a German head appeared above them. At long last the engineers returned with the detonators all primed and wired up.

"Everyone get down!" he yelled, with the entire beach seeming to obey his command.

The Australian soldier twisted the top of the device in his hand and the world was suddenly filled with a monstrous noise that dominated every fibre in James' body, a noise that reminded him of the day when his school had first tested their new electrical fire alarm system. He had been standing there in class when his head, his ears, and his eyes were overwhelmed by an incredible sound that seemed to be coming at him from every direction at once. At the time he had no idea what it was or what it meant, but he was filled with the notion that something immense, that something utterly beyond his comprehension was happening and as he lay there on the coast of Normandy he knew that no matter what else happened in the war, no matter what the outcome was, he had managed to fight his way to the entrance of the Eagle's Nest and leave the world's biggest shit right on its doorstep.

There was a long moment of surreal silence as both sides recovered from the explosion, broken only by what sounded like a gigantic block of ice splitting open. There was a second smaller explosion and suddenly the entire cliff face fell away, crushing and burying anyone who had been above or below it. James could now hear frantic German voices, something that filled him with an eerie fright. After five long years of war, the status of the German soldier had taken on an almost mythical status and, after all this time of fighting from a distance, James wondered if he was mentally prepared to face his seemingly invincible enemy. A German grenade tumbled down the newly-created slope and in the ensuing scramble to get out of its way, the Australian engineer slipped and fell right on top of it; moments later there was a wet and crumpled explosion that filled James with fresh rage. He roared something unintelligible at the top of his lungs and a feeling of empowerment surged though him as the entire Allied force seemed to roar alongside him. Dozens and dozens of men pressed forward, pushing and shoving to be the first one to the top of the cliff, to see what the enemy had done to the world, to be the first one to scream in his face and make him cower in terror.

When James reached the top he was confronted with a baffling array of trenches that crisscrossed in every direction. Over to his left he saw a machine gun nest overlooking the beach below, with three German soldiers firing unrelentingly down at the exposed and vulnerable on-coming soldiers below them. James ran towards the nest, his face contorted with fury, when one of the Germans looked around at him. The soldier's face was young, so incredibly young, a boy of no more than seventeen, his Adam's apple bobbing awkwardly as he swallowed in surprise. There was a look of guilt on his face, one that suggested he had just been caught watching his older sister undressing, and a nervous smile flickered across his face for a brief moment. James fired his rifle with barely a second thought and suddenly the youth was clutching at his throat, writhing around on the floor as a hideous red liquid cascaded through his fingers. A group of British soldiers quickly overwhelmed the gun nest, beating down on the youth and his two comrades with their weapons, with their bayonets, and their bare hands. The clang of metal against metal rang loud in James' ears as trench tools and boots hacked away at the machine gun, silencing it forever. James turned back around and was astonished to see how the entire landscape had changed in the blink of an eye. Hordes of Allied soldiers were swarming across this section, firing at anything and everything that looked like the enemy. A group of Americans came upon a squad of eight German soldiers running along a trench and James felt no pity as they fired their rifles again and again, filling the air with gunfire until the high-pitched *bling!* informed them that their weapons were empty.

James teamed up with some men who were clearing out a set of fortified bunkers. They tossed in grenade after grenade, with every explosion generating round upon round of blood curdling screams, coating the walls with the blood of those who had tried to kill him, a situation that James found himself relishing; these were the bastards who had started the war, the bastards who had chased him back through France and dropped bombs on him as he lay waiting for evacuation at Dunkirk, the bastards who had followed him across the Channel and bombed his town, his city, and his country, the bastards who made him sick with worry every time Mary had to work during an air raid and he wanted to make these same bastards pay for everything they had done. A feeling of completeness settled over him when a soldier with a flamethrower filled the place with fire, turning the bunker into nothing more than a scorched graveyard.

Back outside, James watched as the battle slowly turned into a massacre with German soldiers being mown down without mercy, regardless of whether they were holding a weapon or surrendering with their hands in the air. Corpses were being looted for souvenirs almost the moment they hit the ground, the blood stains still blossoming and clotting on the uniforms, an activity that James himself didn't join in with. Shooting an unarmed man in the middle of a tense battle was one thing, but searching through his pockets afterwards for a memento to remember the occasion by was something that James simply couldn't bring himself to do. Once the sector had been cleared and a beachhead was established, James was astonished at the sheer number of German soldiers that had been taken prisoner; his own personal experience of the battle had given him the impression that every German had been pried from their holes just so they could be shot.

Sitting there on a log under the trees, James suddenly found himself overwhelmed with emotion and his body jerked and convulsed as he buried his head into the crook of his elbow. He sobbed uncontrollably for no more than half a minute but it was a period full of grief, pain, and regret for every terrible thing that the war had forced him to do. Thinking back to his time spent in the barracks after the D-Day landings, he recalled instances of when he thought he could hear the sound of someone sobbing quietly to themselves in the middle of the night; he had always assumed it was due to receiving some bad news of one kind or another, but he understood it better now. James retrieved the photo of Mary from his pocket and once again traced his finger around the outline of her face, doing his best to recall the sound of her voice and the tender softness of her hands. He remained sitting there for a while longer before standing back up to resume his task of collecting some wood for the fire. When the cart was full, the wheels groaned and squealed in protest at being called back into action again and by the time he arrived back at his new home he was perspiring heavily. After checking that the rusty axe wasn't going to fall apart the moment he picked it up, James spent some time chopping up the larger branches he had brought back. He gathered up an armful, leaving the rest for anyone else who might want them and went back into the room he was sharing with David and Piper.

"Hey, I got some more -" he began.

David quickly hushed him and jerked a thumb towards one of the windows. James peered through the glass, not quite able to believe what he was seeing: Piper standing in the middle of the road with over half a dozen young children clapping and cheering at him. One child was climbing around on his back, shouting something down at his friends below. The sound of so many joyous, tiny voices babbling incomprehensibly in French was as bizarre as it was enchanting and adorable.

Bonjour, soldat! Militaire, militaire! Victoire!

Just as one boy stood sharply to attention and saluted in a comically sincere fashion, a brief look of panic flickered across Piper's face as another child tugged enthusiastically at his belt because he wanted to play with the pistol. Piper held the gun well out of reach, released the ammunition clip and handed what was now just a heavy lump of metal to the boy, who gazed at it with wide-eyed fascination and awe.

James found himself conflicted with what he was seeing and it reminded him of one of the reasons why he joined the army in the first place. He had always been fascinated by the power and technology behind tanks, planes, and the floating fortresses of the navy.

36

Whenever he pestered Mary for details about the anti-aircraft guns she worked with, she would tease him by saying he was her "curious little soldier-scholar".

Piper picked up a small girl who had been standing quietly by herself on the side-lines, watching shyly as the boys dominated all the fun. He swirled her around in the air, making airplane noises that had her squealing with delight and the boy with the gun pretended to shoot at her, something that again seemed jarring and strange to James. After witnessing war for himself, it was a sad sight to see children so thrilled and entertained by the prospect of taking part in it for themselves.

"He really is the Pied Piper of bloody Hamelin," observed David. There was a small smile on his face that almost made him look happy.

"Wouldn't it be great to be a kid again, eh?" remarked James, "The whole world's a playground and everyone wants to be your friend."

The smile disappeared from David's face as two aggressive streams of smoke poured out through his nostrils, making him look like a bull that was being prodded and poked with a sharp stick. How was he supposed to know what childhood was like when he had never experienced it? His own father had died when he was five years old and the only memory he had of the man was one of a vague shape looking down at him. By the time he was seven his mother had fallen into the arms of alcoholism, leaving him to fend for himself as a steady stream of strange men began to flow in and out of his house, none of whom seemed to take any interest in his welfare and merely regarded him with suspicion whenever he dared to venture out of his bedroom.

Although he learned to read and write easily enough, the key part of his school education was discovering that people were willing to pay a premium for something if you were the only one who sold it. He would buy sweets from the local shop and sell them for a higher price to anyone who was willing to pay, an act that generated jealousy amongst some boys who took it upon themselves to corner him in an alley one day after school. David knew he was powerless against these four other boys and he burned with rage as he was left with no choice but to hand over his stash and his profits for the day... and just to rub salt into his wounds they decided to give him a good kicking anyway, leaving him to plot revenge and retribution as he lay there bruised and battered on the floor. A few days later he surprised one of his assailants by whacking them across the back of the legs with a stick, before dishing out threefold what had been done to him. He made damned sure that the boy knew who had done it and why he had done it, and over the next few days he paid visits to the other three boys to ensure that they met the same fate as well. Inevitably other enterprising kids decided to get in on the act and it wasn't long before makeshift tuck-shops were springing up in every corner of the school playground. David had predicted that this would happen and he was more than aware that it wasn't really possible for him to put a stop to it - if word got around that he was trying to prevent other people from doing the same thing, there was the risk that they would simply crowd him out so agreements were made about who could sell what and to whom.

Although David's mother passed away when he was thirteen, it wasn't an event that caused him to shed any tears when he received the news. By that time she was little more than a ghost propped up by whisky and vodka bottles, and as the forgotten birthdays and non-existent Christmases mounted up, his emotional attachment to his mother gradually withered away until there wasn't even so much as a sinew of it left. The carpets were dirty and stained with spilt alcohol, whilst the smell of mould made the house unbearable to live in during the summer months and the endless taunts from the older kids at school infuriated him due to his powerlessness to do anything about it. His grandparents took him in after that, something which provided him with a roof over his head but it wasn't a particularly pleasant one - after spending so much time looking after himself and doing whatever he wanted, he resented their attempts at controlling his behaviour and it wasn't long before he developed a habit of running away. Sometimes he came back of his own accord but as time went on it became more and more likely that he would be brought back in the company of a police officer.

James and David continued watching Piper entertain the children. He seemed to do it so effortlessly and tirelessly that it was like watching a stage show magician at the local theatre and whether there were small fingers worming their way into his ears, deft hands trying to sneak their way into his pockets, or cheeky boys slapping his backside, the smile never wavered from Piper's face. Although

James was tempted to go out there and join in with the fun, he felt that he would be an uninvited guest intruding on someone else's party. A dull ache in his arms reminded him of the wood he had brought in.

"Should do us for a while," he remarked, brushing the bark and dirt from his hands, "I'm going to take a walk around the town. Fancy coming? Might be a cafe or something somewhere."

David inhaled the remains of his cigarette and nodded in agreement. He had little else to do and the prospect of a free cup of coffee, whether paid for by James or donated by the grateful local populace, was an appealing prospect. The two of them walked outside and saw that Piper's attention had now turned to three women who had joined the party. It didn't sound like the ladies spoke much English but if their girlish laughter was anything to go by, it seemed that Piper's friendly manner and his affinity with children was perfect for breaking down the language barrier. The only one to notice James and David walking past was the shy little girl who Piper had swished around like an airplane, and she waved enthusiastically at them as they disappeared around the corner. As James smiled and waved back at her, David half-heartedly raised a finger.

For some reason the roads were made up of sections that alternated between stretches of smooth tarmac and large square cobblestones, lending a curious other-worldliness to the place which served to remind James just how far he was from home. Every so often a civilian would wave at them from their window, whereas others would hurry along with their heads down as if they were afraid of being accosted.

40

"Captain weren't joking when he said some of them might be jumpy," remarked David.

"I guess they just need to get used to us."

Two girls approached them, giggling and blushing as they whispered to each other.

"Handsome soldier have name?" the one with blonde hair asked, looking directly at James.

"Um, I'm James," he replied, recognising her as the girl who had kissed him earlier.

"James?" she confirmed, her eyes widening with delight, "Is nice name for handsome man. My name is Angelette," she purred, reaching out for him.

James accepted her hand without even thinking about it and a surge ran up his arm the moment her fingers touched his palm. His hands itched to grab hold of her so he could feel her soft, delicate body pressed up against his own again and he found himself gripping her hand with an unintended ferocity.

"James is strong man," Angelette said as she retrieved her hand back. An element of apprehension passed across her face as if she hadn't expected him to be so rough with her.

Meanwhile, David was doing his best to introduce himself to the other girl who was far shyer and didn't seem to speak English. "David," he told her, making an exaggerated gesture of pointing at himself.

Angelette said something to her friend, who let out another shy giggle.

"Je m'appelle Marie," the other girl said in a small voice.

"Marie, you've got a beautiful name," David told her, a pleasant smile spreading across his face, "and you're beautiful to look at as well."

Angelette said something to her friend again and Marie's face blushed red, something that seemed to please David no end.

"Say, why don't you two come with us?" he suggested, "It'll be great fun."

When Angelette once again said something in French, Marie gasped and covered her mouth with her hand. She looked up at David for a moment before shaking her head.

"David, I am sorry," apologised Angelette, "my friend is shy, maybe next time."

"That's okay. We'll be here a while so there's plenty of time," he replied, eliciting another gasp from Marie as he winked at her.

"We must go now, but we know where you staying and sleeping," Angelette told them. She touched James' hand. "Hope to come visit soon."

The two of them walked off, chattering excitedly in French and casting the occasional glance back at two of the British soldiers who had taken the town by storm. Just before she disappeared round the corner Marie turned around and waved at them, no doubt feeling emboldened by the distance, leaving James and David to stare after her as her exotic voice filled the street.

Au revoir!

David shook his head and smiled at James. "Mate, that blonde one... she couldn't stop looking at you. She's yours whenever you want," his voice was a mixture of envy and admiration.

James pawed at his unshaven face. "I'm engaged," he replied with a small tone of regret.

David shrugged. "So? She's far away in another land and we might be killed tomorrow. Or she might even bump into a nice American GI on her day off..."

James shot him a sharp look.

The flash of anger in James' eyes took David by surprise, reminding him once again that James wasn't the easy mark he once considered him to be. The two of them had joined the army at the same time in 1936 and at nineteen years old they had been the same age as well. Initially he considered James to be the well-schooled but naive and easily-led type, the sort that he had often exploited for his own ends many times over the years. However, in the time since those early days, James seemed to have grown in stature. Was this a result of being exposed to the harsh realities of life during combat? Although the early months of this war had been easy and largely carefree, that all changed once the Germans decided that they were bored of playing around with diplomacy and attacked them in earnest. Suddenly, the life of flirting with young French maids had ended and the retreat back through France began, finishing only with the chaotic evacuation at Dunkirk. After that kind of experience, a man had two choices – lie down and cry or deal with it and come out stronger. David was more than used to dealing with whatever obstacles life threw at him, so he did what he always did and tried not to think about it too much. However, it seemed that the ordeal had awoken something in James that made him stand just that little bit taller and act just that little bit more confident than he had done before, something that became more evident as time went on. Whether this was merely the result of the natural maturing process that a man went through as he crept through his twenties David couldn't possibly say, but he had an inkling that it was the unexpected appearance of a certain girl called Mary that was the catalyst behind it all.

David had met Mary several times and even he had to admit that, in many ways, she was quite a remarkable person. She was attractive, which as far as David was concerned was the most important consideration when it came to deciding whether a woman was worth speaking to or not. He admired her bravery, a trait that he hadn't noticed when he first met her, especially the way she didn't seem to have any qualms about working though her night shifts - whenever the air raid sirens went off David was usually the first one in the queue for the shelters, so he had a grudging respect for Mary's willingness to stay outside scanning the skies for enemy airplanes or delivering supplies in a large truck during a blackout. Mary certainly wasn't shy about her fondness for a glass of wine or two and she could be a lot of fun if she was in the mood for it. Unfortunately, she was just a little bit too intelligent and a little bit too quick-witted for David's tastes and he found himself intimidated when she talked about how she was paid considerably less than her male colleagues, despite the fact that she did the exact same things that they did. Although he didn't necessarily disagree with her point, it was the fact that she spoke so convincingly and confidently about it that unsettled him the most - he preferred being in the company of women who looked up to him as a source of wisdom rather than those who could challenge his way of thinking. And yet despite all this, he had a general idea of why James liked her so much and he could see for himself the difference she had made to him.

Of course this drags out the question of what David actually thought of James. Although he didn't consider him to be a friend, he had developed a kind of respect for him and James was one of the few people that he could trust to one degree or another - he didn't make jokes at his expense and James was one of the few people who had a rough idea of what could be expected of him. Although James outranked him, David knew it was unlikely that he would ever order him to do something that he wouldn't do himself. Much was made of the supposed brotherhood of soldiers, a notion that David scoffed at whenever it was mentioned in his presence, but he considered James to be a very distant cousin-by-marriage that he could tolerate in small doses... or maybe it was simply because James always seemed to have spare cigarettes.

"Don't suppose you've got any -"

"No," interrupted James, shooting him another annoyed look.

David shrugged and looked at something off in the distance.

The two of them came to a small cluster of shops, the first of which was a clothes shop that looked as if it had been closed for quite some time. Two headless mannequins stared forlornly out at them, the clothes hanging limp and deflated from their dust-covered shoulders. A short word had been spelled out in the dirty window but James couldn't tell if it was supposed to be readable to those on the outside or the inside of the building. On the other side of the road was a butcher slicing and chopping up a slab of meat as three women waited patiently in a queue. A young boy was looking curiously up at the row of dead pheasants hanging down from the hooks in the ceiling.

"That's the first time I've ever seen a skinny butcher," remarked David.

A sign with the word *Cafe* printed neatly across it was propped up against the front of a cosy-looking building. A weathered drawing of a steaming cup of coffee hung from the window, presumably to make sure that no-one was confused about what sort of establishment they were about to enter. The door was stiff, causing James to let out grunt as he pushed his way through the entrance and he blinked as his eyes adjusted to the gloomy interior. Behind the counter a typically French-looking barista was busy wiping things down with a damp rag and sitting in a far corner were three customers who filled the air with chatter that was incomprehensible to the ears of most British soldiers. The sound of heavy military boots quickly dominated the room, causing the gossipers to fall silent and the man behind the bar cautiously turned around to greet his new visitors.

"Bon-jaw," James awkwardly blurted out, breaking the silence.

A look of relief appeared on the barista's face. "Eh, eh, you is Brit, yes? You want…?" he stammered, using his hands to imitate someone drinking from a cup.

James tried to hold back a smile as he nodded and mimicked the man's hand signals. The barista came out from behind the counter and ushered the two newcomers towards a table, pulling out two chairs and using his damp cloth to wipe them clean.

"I bring, you sit," he said in broken English, twitching and gesturing as if he were trying to do three things at once.

Although the three customers on another table remained silent, the barista scooted back behind the counter to fill his shop with the *clink* of porcelain and the *swoosh* of hot steam rushing through pipes. A few minutes later he reappeared beside his guests, cups of coffee and plates of sweet pastries balanced expertly in his hands and placed them down in front of them.

"Is for you, is *gratis*," he told them, clapping his hands together and offering a small bow of appreciation.

As he returned to his place behind the counter, one of the French patrons at the other table raised his cup to opportunistically test how far the cafe owner's generosity extended.

Gratis pour moi?

The server made a loud *pffft* noise with his mouth and dismissed the man with a wave of his hand, something that generated a great deal of amusement for the two other men sitting with him.

As James watched this display of French culture with amused curiosity, David was already tucking into his food and making noises of satisfaction. He produced a cigarette from his pocket, leaving James to once again wonder if David was ever as tobacco-poor as he claimed to be. James looked around the room, noting that although at first glance it didn't look too different to any of the cafes he used back home, it was the subtle differences that showed how foreign this land was. The chairs and tables were more ornate, the words on the blackboard behind the counter were French and unfamiliar, and the tiny cups of espresso that everyone seemed to favour over here were in stark contrast to the larger mugs that he was used to seeing... but it was the small Swastika flag hanging from the wall that really compounded the difference. He nudged at David's foot and drew his attention to it.

"Yeah, saw it earlier," he said through a mouthful of pastry, dismissing James' concerns with a shrug. As far as he was concerned the entire continent of Europe was Nazi territory in one form or another and the specifics of the politics were of little interest to him.

The cafe owner caught sight of what his two new visitors were looking at and he became agitated and animated, wagging his finger and vigorously shaking his head to disassociate himself from it.

Non! Non, Non, non!

He tore the flag down and screwed it up into a ball, before spitting on it and tossing it to the floor. He stamped on it a number of times and glanced around anxiously as if he were worried about who might be watching and listening.

"Fuck Hitler!" he said in sharp but somewhat subdued voice.

The three men on the other table murmured in reserved agreement, something that seemed to embolden the owner.

"Fuck Hitler!" he repeated in a louder, more assured voice, much to the delight of his fellow countrymen.

James and David exchanged a glance as the absurdity of this moment, whereby a phrase that was expressed and ventured so often back home had somehow worked its way across the English Channel, through the French countryside and trotted its way into this little coffee shop, sank in. The two of them raised their cups into the air and delighted their Gallic hosts with an enthusiastic "Fuck Hitler!" of their own.

One of the customers decided to try his luck again, lifting his mug in the direction of the owner and repeating the enquiry from a few minutes earlier.

Gratis?

This time the owner laughed and blew a loud raspberry at him.

A few minutes later a woman walked in, visibly struggling with the door as she entered and gestured angrily at it as she approached the counter; the owner shrugged and muttered what was no doubt an oft-repeated apology. James and David finished off the remains of their complimentary meal and stood up to leave. As the owner scurried quickly over to their table to clear away the dishes, David walked over to the side of the counter and snatched up the discarded Nazi flag. The barista gave him a quizzical look, to which David responded by making a scissor motion with his hand.

"Cup of coffee and a nice little souvenir," David remarked once they were back outside, "I'm beginning to like this place." His broad smile turned into a grimace as he realised his thumb was smeared with the cafe owner's saliva.

As they made their way back to their rundown headquarters, they passed two young girls playing in a front garden. One was skipping frantically with a worn old bit of rope, her face bursting with effort and concentration, whilst her friend clapped and chanted encouragement.

Un, deux, trois, quatre, cinque, six, sept, huit, neuf, DIX!

The counting girl let out a shrill scream of delight and rushed forward to embrace her friend, who looked as if she had been perfectly happy to carry on past ten, sending the two of them tumbling to the ground in a heap. As they stood back up and untangled themselves, David raised his hands and gave them a round of applause. The counting girl looked up and seemed unsure, biting nervously at her bottom lip, whereas the other girl, still giddy with adrenaline, took hold of the edges of her dress and did a perfect little curtsey. James laughed, causing the two girls to look at each other and giggle. The shy one followed her friend's lead and performed a curtsey of her own, though it was a reserved and stiff effort. James gave her a polite applause, causing her to blush and laugh from behind the safety of her hand. The bolder girl took a step towards them and asked a question in a language that few British soldiers would understand. James shrugged and answered with a clumsy "Bon-jaw," before smiling and waving, leaving the two girls to stare and wonder if all soldiers used a greeting to say their goodbyes. They resumed their skipping and counting game, filling the empty street with their excitable cries of joy.

By the time James and David arrived back at their temporary barracks it was starting to get dark and the crowd of women and children that had been hanging around earlier was nowhere to be seen. Inside their room, James nearly stepped on Piper's hand as he sat there on the floor cleaning and reassembling his rifle.

"Alright, lads?" he greeted them, leaning back so he didn't get a knee in his face, "been out exploring?"

"Yeah, found a nice little coffee shop not too far away from here," answered James.

"Managed to bump into some nice friendly local girls on the way as well," David added with a grin.

Piper nodded in agreement. "I managed to pick up some of the language from a couple of experts: oon, der, twois, sink, sat..." his voice trailed off as he tried to recall the words, "well, it's something like that anyway."

Piper resumed working on his rifle, something that filled James with the same kind of fascination he experienced whenever he saw tanks charging across a field or planes roaring down the runway; although he didn't possess the skill or the expertise to work those machines himself, he loved learning the technical details about them. Arranged neatly on a cloth in front of Piper was a spectacular array of clips, springs, and strangely-shaped bands of metal that looked more like a schoolboy project than the individual components of an instrument of death.

Piper diligently wiped down each part with a second cloth that was covered with grubby smudges of black grease, before carefully slotting them back into place.

"She's a vain old thing, is my dear Pipe," Piper explained with a twinkle in his eye, "likes to be stroked, cleaned, and massaged to keep her in tip-top condition."

"Maybe you should treat her to a new dress," suggested James, pointing at the old rag that was poking out of Piper's chest pocket.

"Nah, she needs a bit of muckiness to keep her on her toes."

"Treat 'em mean, keep 'em keen," agreed David.

Piper's grin widened, once again exposing the gap in his teeth. "Davey Boy knows what I'm talking about," he remarked with a small nod of his head. He swung the rifle around and pointed the butt towards David. "You can spank her arse if you fancy a treat before bedtime."

David frowned, appreciating neither the nickname nor what he considered to be a mocking of his sexuality. "No, thanks," he replied flatly.

"What's it like?" James asked, "Being a sniper, I mean."

Piper placed his rifle carefully on the ground and thought for a moment. "You may as well ask me what it's like to bayonet someone in the stomach; it's just part of being a soldier."

"No, that's not the same," disagreed James, "with hand to hand combat I'm fighting for my life, but a sniper is shooting at people who don't even know they're there."

Piper shrugged. "Same for a bomber pilot. The people on the ground don't know he's there either."

"Nah, that's not the same thing either," James persisted, "the bomber pilot is dropping stuff on a city. He doesn't ever see the faces of the people below him."

David was now listening to this exchange with interest, though he chose to remain silent as he lit up another cigarette.

Piper shrugged again. "It depends what I'm actually doing. If I'm just one more soldier in support of a larger force then I don't really get time to think about who I'm firing at because there's so many of them. I just aim at a body, pull the trigger, and move on to the next one, no different to what either of you two might do."

He scratched at his face and grimaced. "The harder part is if I'm supposed to lie in wait for a specific target. I might be sent somewhere in a jungle or the middle of a forest and have to wait hours or maybe even days for them to come along. I have to remain as still as possible so I don't give myself away. If I need a crap, I have to slowly roll over onto my side and do it in a bit of cloth and take it back with me."

James raised his eyebrows in surprise. He had always assumed being a sniper was a relatively simple affair that needed nothing other than a keen pair of eyes and a steady hand. However, as fascinating as this was it still wasn't really answering what he wanted to know.

"But that moment when you look down the sight and you're looking right at them..."

Piper scratched at the back of his head as he grasped for the words to answer the question and when he did speak, his face was sombre. "Sometimes they'll be looking right at me without even knowing it. I'll be able to see the scars on their face or maybe even the dirt under their fingernails when they shove a cigarette in their mouth…"

As James listened intently, David looked down at his own hands and cast an anxious glance out of the window.

"…and it can be a bit weird sometimes, especially if they're in civilian clothing. When it comes to actually pulling the trigger, the adrenaline will be pumping so I don't really think about it too much. And once I've actually shot them everything suddenly changes because I've got to get away as fast as possible, so again I don't really get a chance to think about it.

"It's usually in the days afterwards that I start to play it back in my mind. It's easier to think of them as being evil men if they're in uniform; anyone who goes to work wearing the skull and crossbones on their shoulder is a bit funny in the head if you ask me. But sometimes I'll think back and realise that they had a similar taste in clothes to me, or recall that they had a big gap in their teeth."

Piper used his finger to push his top lip up, exposing his missing tooth in a way that made James feel uncomfortable. "How would you feel about shooting someone who went to the same dentist as you?"

James nodded slowly as he took this all in, causing Piper to let out a snort.

"Yeah, I bet you never thought of it like that. Sometimes I just see it as a job that will help end the war and make life better for everyone, whereas other days I realise those men had families like everyone else," he let out a sigh and shot James a quick smile, "I bet you wish you hadn't asked, right?"

"You could say that, yeah," James confessed, "makes me wish I'd joined the tank division."

"Nah, I wish I'd signed up as a chef," chuckled Piper, "mind you, I'd probably end up poisoning everyone with my bad cooking."

The two of them sensed that the conversation had come to an end and the room fell largely silent, broken only by the sound of soldiers in heavy boots moving around elsewhere in the building. David took it upon himself to get a fire going, filling the air with the clunk of sticks being tossed into a fireplace and the sparks from his lighter were as bright as a camera flash in the dark room. Once the fire was burning nicely James searched around in his pocket for the photograph of Mary. In the gloomy light of the flickering flames her expression seemed to shift and change like a retreating cloud during a thunderstorm, making her look sad, hopeful, and melancholic all at once. It reminded him of one particular time when she had been working on a night shift and he had gone to bed without her. Usually she was as quiet as a mouse when she entered the house, but on this occasion he had been woken by the sound of the front door being slammed shut. Her footsteps were unusually heavy as she made her way up the stairs, causing James to wonder if he was having an absurd nightmare about an overnight German invasion. He opened his eyes just as she entered the room and there were two dull thuds followed by a flap of cloth as she kicked off her shoes and threw her jacket into the corner.

"James, you awake?" she asked. Her voice sounded strained and tired, caught somewhere in between anger and sadness.

Although James could only answer with a sleepy grunt, it served to answer her question and Mary crawled across the bed and huddled up next to him.

"One of my friends was killed tonight," she said, letting out a mournful sigh. "Flew right into the side of a hill after getting lost in bad weather. She didn't stand a chance."

At first James had no idea who Mary was talking about until he realised she must be referring to someone from the Air Transport Auxiliary. The ATA was most notable for the civilian pilots who ferried new airplanes from the factories to the airfields or flew damaged aircraft from the airfields to the scrap yards, an important job that allowed the RAF pilots to concentrate on combat duty. A large number of these ATA pilots were female, which was a source of consternation amongst the sections of society who didn't think women were capable of operating anything more complicated than a saucepan.

"I took the phone call just as my shift finished," Mary continued, "I *knew* I shouldn't have answered it, that blasted thing only ever rings to deliver bad news."

James was more awake now and he rolled over so he could pull her closer to him. She was still wearing her uniform but he could feel her shaking with rage beneath the thin fabric.

"I'm sorry," he told her, kissing her on the forehead, "I've lost lots of friends to this war as well. It's horrible."

Mary took a deep breath and let out a long sigh. "James, you boys get all the training and all the equipment that you need and no-one tries to blame you if something goes wrong. These girls who deliver the planes... they have to fly in bad weather that not even the RAF pilots will go up in, despite not having anyone to show them what all the different instruments and controls do."

James didn't have anything to say in response to this so he stroked her cheek with his hand, finding her face to be hot and wet with tears.

"I hung around for a while afterwards so I could let the others know as well. The phone rang a second time and I jumped at it in case it turned out that she was still alive," she said, taking another deep breath. "James, they're trying to pin all the blame on her, saying that she shouldn't have been flying or that the weather wasn't really as bad as the reports say it was. I was so angry that I slammed the phone down and drove straight home in one of those big trucks, blackout be damned."

"That's outrageous," James told her, raising his voice in disgust. "Everyone's under pressure to do long hours for the war effort, they can't blame people when mistakes happen like that."

"Yes," agreed Mary, "and some of us have to do it for half the credit as well. Is someone going to blame me if I get killed because an engineer didn't screw one of the big guns down properly?"

A surge of anger rushed through James, causing him to tense up and grip her tightly for a moment. "If anyone tries something like that," he growled, "I'll court martial the bastard myself."

Mary let out a quick halting laugh of relief. "Oh, James, you're such a sweetie. What would I do without you? Where would I be without my brave soldier?" She shuffled closer to him and rested her head on his chest. "Where would I be?" she repeated softly.

James lay there in the dark stroking her cheek and swirling his fingers around her damp face. After a few minutes he felt her grip on him slacken and her breathing settled down to a more regular rhythm as exhaustion began to take hold of her. He continued running his hand across her soft skin, stopping only when he too fell asleep.

The fire flared up briefly, once again turning the photograph into a living entity as the shadows were banished from the room and for a moment it was as if Mary were sitting there in the room with him, flashing him that girlishly vulnerable smile that appeared every so often.

"Hey," interrupted Piper, "I recognise that look."

It took James a few moments to realise who he was talking to. "Sorry, what?"

"Gazing at that photo you looked like you were in heaven."

James smiled sheepishly.

"No need to be embarrassed," Piper reassured him, "though the question on everyone's lips is whether you're looking at a picture of your dog or your wife."

As David snorted with laughter, a look of momentary shock appeared on James' face.

Piper held his hands up in mock surrender. "Sorry, couldn't resist it. Mind if I have a quick look at her?"

A pulse of jealousy flashed through James as he was once again reminded of how far away he was from home. Although the photo was little more than a dog-eared piece of paper, handing it over to someone else felt akin to letting another man share her bed for the night. He held Piper's gaze for a moment before relenting.

"Here," he said, feeling like a plucked chicken as Piper took it from him.

As David also leaned in for a look, Piper let out a low whistle of admiration. "She's a corker alright. No wonder you always gaze at her like a lovesick puppy."

James smiled. "We're engaged to be married," he explained, as if to remind them that she was already spoken for.

"Yeah, I'll bet. If there's one thing worth fighting and keeping yourself alive for, it's a good woman's hand in marriage."

As James patiently waited for the return of the photo, David looked up and shot him a quick wink. Piper flipped the picture over, presumably looking for a lover's message rather than the back of a girl's head, before handing it back.

"What about you, Piper? You must have an entire family waiting for you back home."

Piper glanced awkwardly down at the floor. "Well, I'm pretty sure they're waiting for me somewhere, but I know they're not waiting at home," he raised his hand and pointed a finger towards the ceiling, "they're waiting somewhere special."

It took James a heartbeat to grasp what Piper meant and he raised his eyebrows in surprise. "Sorry, I had no idea," he apologised.

"Nah, no need to apologise, it was me who started talking about other people's business."

There was a short silence. "So, um, what happened?"

"Killed by a German bomb, right near the start of the war. We lived out in one of the quieter towns and hardly anyone had a bomb shelter back then. Most people thought a little ditch in the back garden would be enough, until a stray bomber happened to drop his load on our heads," Piper looked up at James, "there wasn't much left to bury afterwards either."

David let out a stream of smoke from his mouth, slowly and quietly as if he was afraid of inadvertently interrupting anyone.

"Katherine was her name," Piper continued, "always wanting to do things for others. She ran her own Girl Guide group and had them doing all sorts of stuff. One week she set them a goal of doing ten good deeds every month as part of their badge work and it wasn't long before the girls were running around knocking on people's doors, asking if they needed help with the gardening or the cleaning," he smiled to himself, "they drove everyone mad after a while, pestering complete strangers for jobs that might need doing."

Piper rubbed at his mouth before continuing. "Remember when all those Jewish refugee children started arriving from Europe just before the war started? A few of them got housed up near us. Poor little sods, they were frightened to death and barely spoke any English. Well, when Katherine heard about them she enrolled them into the Guide group so they could make some friends."

He looked up at James, spreading his hands. "But how'd you get kids to be friends if they can't speak to each other?"

James answered with a shrug, causing Piper to let out a small laugh.

"Yeah, that's what I said but Katherine came up with the idea of teaching them Morse Code. It was for another one of their badges so it fit right into everything else and they could all join in with it," Piper shook his head, "can you believe it? Teaching Morse bloody Code to kids."

"Clever idea, that," James said, sounding genuinely impressed.

"Yeah, she was great for that. If a kid came to her with a problem, she'd always be able to come up with an answer that made sense to them. When the children from the cities were evacuated to the country towns, she had her girls all dressed up in their uniforms waiting for them at the train station to hand out drinks and sandwiches."

"She's special," James told him in earnest, "I'm talking one in a thousand special. And she chose you, that's something to be proud of."

"Yeah, she was," Piper agreed, "she really was."

"I saw you playing around with those kids earlier. It looked like you were continuing in her footsteps."

"Nah," Piper flattened his palm out and held it two feet above the floor, "every little kid I see, boy or girl, reminds me of my little John. He was always laughing and smiling, which was the best thing to come home to after spending all day listening to a staff sergeant shouting his head off."

"Sounds like we had the same staff sergeant," James quipped.

Piper continued as if he hadn't heard anyone say anything. "Every time I get those kids laughing... it's almost like if I keep them happy, my little John will just appear next to me, safe and sound," he remained silent for a moment. "And I swear, the only thing that kept me going up that damned beach was the idea that if the war ended the day afterwards, I'd be able to go home and everything would be back to how it was."

Although David had been listening to Piper's story he had been content to just stare at the fire and watch as the flames slowly ate their way through the logs. His ears had pricked up towards the end and he was more than aware of which beach Piper was talking about. In fact there wasn't a single survivor of D-Day who wouldn't immediately know which beach it was that Piper was referring to... well, providing you ignored the few who looked as if they were going to end up in a mental asylum.

David remembered the journey across the Channel, crammed down below decks and packed in with everyone else, the doorways and corridors filled with so many men, boots, and equipment that it made him nervous. He had tried to wangle himself a place on one of the upper decks but he was beaten to it by people who had far sharper elbows than even he possessed, leaving him with little more than an uncomfortable wooden bench to sit on. As the Allied Armada worked its way across the water David's world rocked gently from side to side, an unsettling motion that felt unnatural and left him at the mercy of whoever was doing the driving. He felt trapped every time he glanced over at the door, knowing that he would quickly get lost amongst the maze of narrow corridors and stairways if there was an emergency. An aggravating *plick plick plick* sound reached his ears, filling him with an odd revulsion when he realised that someone was clipping their fingernails. David fumbled around in his pocket for a cigarette and was soon working his way through the entire packet, inhaling and savouring each puff as if he could store them all up for later. Just as the nicotine was starting to make him feel light headed, a small shudder went through the ship as the engines were shoved into reverse, filling him with the kind of nervous anxiety that a budding actor might feel just before their first audition. He gasped when the sudden shriek of a whistle broke him from his thoughts, sending his cigarette tumbling to the floor where it was quickly flattened by dozens of flat-footed soldiers. The air was filled with the stomp and clatter of an entire army on the move and David was powerless as it dragged him through a confusing array of doorways, passages, and ramps, before shoving him out into the loading bays. Someone shouted and pointed him towards one of the landing craft, dismay consuming him when he realised that he was stuck right up at the front, the most dangerous place it was possible to be. Just as the landing craft started heading out it had to swerve to avoid colliding with another one and David took advantage of the resulting confusion by shoving his way towards the back.

Once the chaos had been sorted out, the craft's engines roared into life and the trip towards the shore resumed in earnest. The disturbing sound of what could have been a large animal clearing its throat filled the air as someone emptied the contents of their stomach all over their boots, the stale and salty stench of the sea mixing in with the smell of vomit, a mixture that worked its way up David's nostrils and down into his belly. His vision began to cloud over as he was reminded of the aroma of a fish market, a place he had hated ever since his mother had once tried to cook kippers on Christmas Day; the obnoxious smell had driven him outside into the freezing cold snow, but not before he had emptied his guts all over the kitchen floor. Standing there in the landing craft, David suddenly bent over and groaned as his stomach contracted and squeezed itself empty. He sagged against the metal wall to his left, taking in deep breaths as he struggled to regain control of himself. Sea spray surged over the side, causing his teeth to chatter even as the sweat tumbled down his face. He glanced across the water and made eye contact with someone in another craft, nodding involuntarily as a moment of distant soldierly cousinhood filled him with a rare sense of belonging.

As the craft slowed down, David swallowed hard and gripped his rifle as he thought back to all the training drills they had endured for this moment. There was going to be a loud clang as the front locking bolt was released, and the clanking of cogs and chains spinning themselves free would rattle through his bones as the ramp yawned itself open and slammed down onto the beach... but something was wrong. Instead of charging forward, everyone around him was collapsing as if someone were smashing their shins with a sledgehammer and the inside of the craft was suddenly alive and sparkling like a Christmas tree as bullets bounced and ricocheted off the sides. A survival instinct kicked in and David heaved himself over the edge without even thinking about it, an act that seemed to take an eternity as the world slowed down to a crawl. He found himself tumbling through the air, the sea looming towards him like a gigantic monolith, before finally plunging into the depths of the English Channel. The taste of seaweed and the stench of the ocean oozed between his teeth and filled his mouth, his throat, and his stomach, pulling him down and enveloping him in a blanket of freezing cold confusion. He wormed and wriggled his fingers underneath the straps of his backpack, desperate to shed the deadly weight that was conspiring to drag him down to the centre of the earth. Something zipped past his head that could have been a fish or a bullet; his foot kicked against something smooth and hard that could have been a stone or someone's forehead; his teeth bit down on something that could have been a bit of seaweed or the sodden remains of a cigarette. He felt something snatching and grabbing at his collar, something that wouldn't go away no matter how much he tried to fight against it, something that was pulling and tugging at him, until suddenly he burst above the surface and his feet found solid ground. He took a few faltering steps forward before collapsing onto his hands and knees, sea water and vomit cascading from his mouth. As his fingers dug into the wet sand, a wave washed over him, a wave that was as red as exposed flesh and filled his mouth with the coppery taste of blood.

Somehow he managed to crawl and stumble his way over to a group of soldiers sheltering behind a tank trap, an ugly metal contraption that seemed to have spontaneously sprouted out from the ground just so it could tower over him. Out of the corner his eye he could see someone staring at him, someone whose eyes were wide with fear and terror, someone who wanted answers and to be told what to do next. David ignored him for as long as he could, not wanting to be responsible for anyone or to have anyone depending on him for survival, when he realised that the eyes were vacant and empty rather than helpless and desperate. A clump of soldiers began moving up the beach and David followed them, doing his best to make sure that he was never at the front. They passed a wounded soldier lying in a shell hole clutching at his side and screaming out for help, and David watched in amazement as a medic appeared from nowhere to treat him, an act of selflessness that struck him as alien and absurd. He found himself sheltering behind a sandbank with a few dozen other soldiers, a number that seemed pathetically small when he thought back to how many men had been crammed into the ships such a short time ago. Every second felt like a constant fight for survival, with men shouting and screaming for help, guns being discharged on a whim, and no-one seemed to know what was going on. He didn't recognise any of the faces or any of the voices around him and men shouted at him in strange accents from all over the British Isles, some of them angry, some of them pleading, but most of them filled with terror.

Somehow the German defences were finally breached, though David had no idea how it had happened nor how many men had been killed in the process. He attached himself to a group of Welsh and Scottish soldiers who seemed content to leave most of the heroics to everyone else, preferring to focus on the easier targets. They infiltrated a small bunker and David was confronted by a startled soldier who threw his arms into the air and shouted something in a foreign language.

Kapitulation!

David stood there staring at him for a moment, not quite able to believe that he was finally in this position. Four long years had passed since the Germans had chased and hounded him from the continent and the entirety of that time flashed across his mind in an instant. All the devastation that had been wrought upon his town, all the sacrifices that had been forced upon him, the grinding tedium of rationing, the relentless bombardment of government propaganda, all of it had been squeezed into a microdot that was only now being presented to him... yet David couldn't find it in himself to actually hate this German soldier who was cowering before him. The Nazi state had taken over most of Europe, conquering and plundering at a whim, providing its military forces with everything that they could possibly need, yet this pathetic excuse for a man was giving up the moment the going got tough.

Kapitulation!

David's expression was entirely passive as he pulled the trigger of his rifle, feeling nothing but contempt as the sound of gunfire bounced off the walls and roared back at him. The soldier flopped to the floor and David stood staring at him for a moment, not quite able to believe how easy it had been, and fired at him again just to make sure. He bent down and began sifting through the German's pockets, his hands eagerly feeling around for potential prizes and souvenirs. Bits of paper and photographs were quickly discarded whilst medals, scarves, a watch, and a Luger pistol put a big smile on his face. When David stood back up again he heard cheering and laughter coming from another room.

"Hey, London!" a burly Scottish soldier addressed him, "have a wee peek at the German lasses that're waiting for us."

David frowned, not appreciating the nickname. He took the photo that was being offered to him and found himself looking into the smiling face of a young girl who couldn't have been any more than twenty years old. Despite the pretty face she looked utterly unremarkable and wouldn't seem out of place in any town that David had been to back home. There were no Swastikas, no aggressive snarls, no guns, and no black uniforms anywhere in the picture... it was just a happy innocent looking girl who wasn't ever going to see her fiance again.

David stared at the picture for a moment longer before handing it back. "Maybe you should write her a letter."

"Aye, I should," boomed the Scot, boisterously clapping David on the shoulder, "write her a wee poem about two war lovers meeting up in Berlin."

No matter how jovially it was intended, David didn't appreciate being manhandled or slapped so he just smiled half-heartedly as the rest of the men laughed loudly at the joke. A number of German soldiers were lying on the ground, every one of them dead, their smart uniforms unbuttoned and their arms contorted into absurd poses from the looting. David thought he spotted something and he bent down to slide back a sleeve on one of the corpses, revealing a nice brass watch. He smiled and unhooked the timepiece with ease, generating a look of jealous annoyance from one of the others.

David lifted up his prize and let it dangle teasingly from his hand. "Finders, keepers," he reminded them all.

The burly Scot let out a harsh laugh. "London, you've got a mean streak alright."

In the warm makeshift headquarters, David sat there staring at the logs shifting and crackling as the flames gradually consumed them. His jaw was slack and his mouth hung open, cigarette smoke slowly tumbling out from between his lips as he remembered how shocked he had been to discover how ripped and holed his uniform had been after D-Day. When he stripped down in the medic tent his body had been covered in bruises, cuts, and shrapnel wounds that seemed to have sprung up from nowhere. How many times had he been in the gun sights of a German soldier that day? How much did he owe his survival to sheer luck? A sharp bee-sting sensation in his hand snapped him from his thoughts and when he looked down he saw that his cigarette had burnt down to his fingers. He tossed it into the fire in annoyance, briefly wondering why he bothered with such a stupid habit in the first place. David slid his hand underneath the sleeve of his uniform and felt around his wrist for the silver German watch that he was wearing. It was one of the first souvenirs he had obtained in France five years ago and it was a favourite that he had grown quite attached to. Unlike many of the cheap watches that were sold in British shops, this one never seemed to lose the time and hardly ever needed winding up. Although he didn't think much of their foreign policy, David had to give the Nazis credit for their ability to consistently produce such high quality gifts. He ran his index finger in an anti-clockwise circle around the face of the watch, savouring how impeccably smooth the polished surface was. As ridiculous as it sounded, David had come to view this particular watch as something of a good luck charm, something that acted as a focal point for all the struggles he had endured throughout his life - it was a survivor just like he was, battling against adversity, outliving its peers, and even being prepared to switch allegiances if the situation called for it.

Although David hadn't changed sides in quite the same way that his favourite souvenir had, he had nonetheless dabbled on the wrong side of the law for many years before joining the army... and he still did if the circumstances were right. As he entered his late teens, David realised that the only way he was going to escape the shackles of his grandparents was if he secured himself a regular income and found himself a place of his own to live in. However, after discovering that the demands of employment came with burdens he wasn't willing to put up with - having to turn up on time each morning was a particular bugbear of his, as was being expected to socialise with his co-workers - it wasn't long before he was once again relying on unsavoury methods in order to make money. As time went on, those unsavoury methods increasingly crossed over into the downright illegal and he found himself in the company of unpleasant individuals and gangs. Initially he was involved with relatively simple scams such as distracting people so that someone else could steal their wallet or handbag, but it wasn't long before he was handling large amounts of stolen goods and taking part in more complicated schemes that required people who could think on their feet. As he became more attached to these underground gangs, he found himself coming under the watchful eye of the police and the amount of overnight stays in cells began to stack up. Often avoiding lengthy periods in prison only by the skin of his teeth, David became increasingly worried about the direction his life was taking him in. A gang who were looking for people to take part in a kidnapping approached him to see if he was interested, something that set alarm bells ringing in his head. The money was good - very good - but abducting people was an unpleasant business that he really didn't want to be involved with. In fact anything that carried a punishment of having to pay a visit to the hangman's gallows was something that he wanted to give a wide berth and by the time he was nineteen, David realised that he was inching closer and closer to the edge of a cliff that would leave him tumbling down into the abyss if he didn't sort himself out. One day he walked past the local town hall and noticed a new sign leaning up against the wall.

Your country needs you!
Join the army and see the world!
Enquire within.

Ordinarily he scoffed at the idea of anyone falling for such obvious propaganda nonsense: as far as he was concerned, the army was for people who couldn't fend for themselves and needed someone to tell them what to do all the time. However, the sign was still there the next day... and the day after that... and by the time a fortnight had gone by David had begun giving it some serious consideration. As much as he hated the idea of having to obey orders, the prospect of spending long periods of his life in prison was even worse and the army offered him the opportunity of a regular wage, a stable environment, and an existence that was considered socially acceptable. He might even get posted somewhere nice and warm like North Africa or Singapore, away from the dreary British weather, away from all the trouble that was brewing in Europe, away from... well, everyone. There would be no officers of the law wanting to feel his collar, no gangs pestering him to do their dirty work, and no ghosts from his past to worry about.

When his application into the military was finally accepted, David was only partly relieved. A voice in the back of his head was telling him that he was making a huge mistake and he would be shot for desertion within a year, a voice that he had trouble silencing and one that he wished he had listened to when basic training started. His days suddenly changed from being empty and dull with brief periods of danger to being full of shouting, running, firing weapons, more shouting, drills, and crawling underneath barbed wire as someone shouted at him. Each night he lay in bed, his body sore and aching, wondering how anyone could put up with such a ridiculous lifestyle. However, after the first couple of weeks, things gradually started to get better and each day was slightly easier than the one that had preceded it. He also began to appreciate the clean bed that was always ready and prepared for him, the regular hot meals that he didn't have to cook himself, the secure roof over his head... not to mention the fact that he was getting paid a liveable wage on top of all this. Although he kept himself to himself for the most part, tolerating the company of everyone else only when he had to, a fellow trainee called James Bowden was someone he came to trust after a while; a presence that made his early military life a little bit more bearable.

That's not to say he had left his unsavoury work behind him entirely. With war breaking out across Europe, the British armaments industry was tasked with ramping up production as the military sought to expand its stockpile of weapons. Small arms like pistols were always in demand and David earned a small amount of cash by selling them to anyone who was willing to pay the price. The main difference was that his army income gave him the luxury to be able pick and choose what nefarious activities he got involved in, rather than having to rely on them to survive.

The fire was now down to little more than glowing embers, leaving the room in a state of almost complete darkness. David glanced around and saw that his two roommates were already stretched out on the floor fast asleep. He turned back to the fire and used his boot to shift the remains of the logs around, before settling himself down for the night. Out through the window, David looked up at the moon with a feeling of distrust. No matter where in the world he went and no matter what job he was doing, that damned celestial body was always staring ominously down at him like the world's most persistent policeman. The only respite he ever seemed to get was when it was cloudy but even then the relief was only fleeting and temporary - there was always a small gap for it to peer through or maybe even a change in the weather that could bring it out again.

A faint noise started up in the distance, one that David quickly recognised as the steady *crump* of artillery fire, reminding him that no matter how comfortable he allowed himself to get the war was never far away. He felt under his sleeve and circled his finger around the face of his watch a few times before turning away from the window and letting himself fall asleep.

***

Chapter Three

James was once again awoken the next morning by one of Piper's belches, an unpleasant noise that spoiled the last few moments of a particularly pleasant dream he had been enjoying.

"Another rude awakening?" Piper asked, his grin exposing the missing tooth.

James sat up and grunted, glancing around the room to get his bearings. "What... what time is it?"

Piper shrugged. "Dunno. But it's another day of not being shot at, so may as well get up and make the most of it."

James considered this for a moment and quickly decided it was the sort of day that was ideal for catching up on his sleep. He lay back down and drifted off again, doing his best to ignore Piper's mutterings behind him. Half an hour later he was startled awake again when David stomped into the room and dumped an armful of wood next to the fireplace.

"Some plonker left a load of it out back" he proudly exclaimed, brushing the dirt from his hands, "thought I'd grab it before anyone else did."

James sat up as he realised that he wasn't going to get any more sleep at this rate. He looked at the wood David had brought in and smiled to himself before going upstairs to the bathroom. Having a wash in a proper sink was something of a luxury and he decided that the best means of taking advantage was to have a shave. Although the sound of heavy boots on bare floorboards made it hard to fully believe, if he squinted and did his best to shut out the noise it was almost like he was back home in his own bathroom. He rinsed the razor in the sink and when he looked back up into the mirror he half-expected to see the reflection of Mary standing there in the doorway looking and smiling at him. The two of them worked shifts so there would be some weeks where they hardly got to see each other, with one of them leaving as the other one was coming in. This meant they took full advantage of every free moment they had together; she relished his soldierly physique as much as he craved the softness of her breasts and the smoothness of her thighs, and she had developed a habit of pouncing on him just after he had finished shaving. When this lack of free time was coupled with the fact that the two of them were each bringing in a fairly reasonable wage, it meant that financially they were better off than many others were and they could afford to rent their own place together. Of course, many conservative types frowned at their living arrangements and weren't shy about voicing their disapproval.

"Oh, hush you stupid old buzzard!" Mary had once admonished a particularly persistent critic. "Who do you think it is that keeps those guns going when you're safe underground in your shelter each night? If I want to live in bloody sin, then I sodding well will!"

James splashed his face with water and used his hands and his reflection to make sure he hadn't missed anything in the harder to reach spots, before making his way back downstairs and going around the rear of the building for a bit of peace and quiet. He noticed that the rusty axe and the dilapidated cart were still where he had left them the day before, waiting patiently in the hope that someone would deem them important enough to be used again. James turned around and took a few slow strides towards the trees, content to admire the pleasant scenery for a while. After a few minutes, a noise from behind him caused his entire body to tense as he snapped his head round.

"Oh, sorry!" a pretty blonde girl apologised, "I no mean to startle you."

James relaxed and tried to recall her name. "Angelette? That's okay, you just surprised me."

She took a few more steps and stood next to him, looking out across the horizon as he had been doing. "You like out here?"

He nodded. "Yeah. Nice and peaceful, almost like I'm in another world."

"Is right, yes. I often come here in summer, maybe take walk through woods. I have happy memories of here, used to play as child. Climb trees, roll in grass, make camp in tents... was lots of fun."

James looked at her with amusement, not quite able to picture her doing those things. "I never had you down as a tomboy," he remarked.

A look of confusion appeared on Angelette's face. "Is what? Boy of... I not know that word."

James laughed. "Sorry. It's hard to imagine you doing all those boy things, you look too, um..." he tried to catch himself before he said too much, wary of giving her an excuse to start getting overly friendly again.

She smiled coyly, something that sent an unwelcome warm rush through James when she finished the sentence for him. "Too grown up?"

"What was this building used for?" he asked, changing the subject.

She shrugged and absently fiddled with some jewellery on her wrist. "Not really sure. My papa, I know he used to chop up wood for people who used building. I think that his axe."

There was a moment of silence between them until she looked up at James. "You have had shave."

When she reached out and stroked his cheek, a pulse of lust ran through him as her soft fingers melted on his face. All at once he was aware of the smell her perfume, of the outline of her breasts beneath that close-fitting dress, of her beautiful white neck that he wanted to kiss and caress forever. The hungry look on his face was all too plain for her to see and she stepped forward to kiss him on the lips. James didn't hesitate to pull her towards him, craving her femininity, her warmth, and her softness, his hands desperate to grab and squeeze at every part of her body. She welcomed him without pause, bringing her arms up around his neck, the bangles on her arms clanging loudly and jarringly next to his ear.

Bling!

James was filled with horror and revulsion as her tongue suddenly felt like a shredded lump of intestine in his mouth, her perfume nothing more than the smell of cordite and explosives. He pulled back, his eyes wild and tormented, shoving her away from him and taking several deep breaths.

"What...?" she asked, looking hurt and surprised.

James blinked and glanced around him, getting control of himself again. "No, I... I'm engaged to be married, I can't do this."

"Oh," replied Angelette, sounding disappointed, "but she is far away."

"Yes," James lamented. "She's very far away. Too far away."

He reached into his pocket and pulled out the photo of Mary, thrusting it at Angelette in the same way that a superstitious person might wield a crucifix to ward off an evil spirit. "Here, look. Her name is Mary."

Angelette reluctantly took the photo. "She very pretty," she admitted after a few moments, "what she do in England?"

James searched for answer that would make sense. "She shoots down German planes."

"Really?" she queried, sounding impressed, "Fight and kill Germans? She sound very brave."

James smiled. "Yes, she is. Probably braver than me sometimes."

Angelette traced her finger gently across the face of the photo. "When Germans came here, they do terrible things to us. Take from shops without pay, push us around, steal our food..." she glanced away for a moment, "...harass the women as well. One man told German to leave his daughter alone, which made soldier very angry. Next day, German get in tank and drive to this man's house and fired big gun at it. House was destroyed but lucky no-one was inside."

"I'm sorry, I had no idea," sympathised James, "my town was bombed by the Germans and lots of people lost their homes."

"Yes, very sad. But you fight back and bomb German cities in revenge. I wanted to fight but too scared and not know how. I think about maybe put poison in their food, but everyone else too scared as well," Angelette looked up at him, "I bet if Mary here she show us how to fight."

James let out a small laugh. "Yes, she would. She really would. And even if no-one else joined in, she'd probably do it all by herself."

"I like to meet her one day. You come back after war maybe?"

"Maybe," James cautiously agreed. Merely surviving the war was a far-off dream and only a fool would assume it was a certainty. Even if he *did* survive, James wasn't sure if he would ever want to leave his house let alone cross the Channel again.

Angelette handed the photo back, which James was happy to reclaim. As he put it back into his pocket an idea entered his head.

"Ever fired a gun before?" he asked, holding his pistol out for her.

"No," she replied in a small voice, looking at the new object in his hand as if it were a poisonous snake.

"Here, take it," he told her. "You'll need a weapon if you want to fight."

She gingerly took it from him. "Is cold and heavy," she observed.

"Hey, careful," he advised, stepping behind her. "Don't point it at someone unless you're going to fire it."

James spent a minute showing her how to hold the gun and suggested that she had a go at actually firing it.

"What should I shoot?" she asked innocently.

James shrugged and pointed at something in the distance. "Try those trees."

Angelette raised the pistol and stood in a stiff shooting stance as she braced herself for the kickback. James found himself thinking how absurd this was, a pretty blonde girl in a dress, her face covered in cosmetics and lipstick, standing there practicing how to –

The sound of a gunshot suddenly filled the air, bouncing and echoing off the ground, the buildings, and the trees. James merely blinked but he had to be quick to reach out for his student who was stumbling back in surprise and shock. The weapon fell from her hands and clattered to the ground, causing James to step away just in case it went off again.

Angelette covered her face with her hands and said some words that James didn't understand. "No, no, I... I can't do it again, is not for me," she stammered, looking petrified.

James picked the pistol up and placed it back into the holster, trying to hide a small smile.

"You think I am a silly girl, yes? I feel silly but wish I was brave like Mary."

James shrugged. "I was pretty nervous the first time I used a gun. Most people are."

Angelette nodded. "May I see photo again?"

James hesitated before handing it over, wondering if she was going to drop that as well.

She traced a finger across the picture. "Yes, I see it now. She has brave face that is full of strength."

Angelette stepped forward and took James' hand in hers and squeezed it. "You are lucky man to have her and she lucky to have man like you. You will survive war and go back home and get married. Have lots of children, big happy family."

Her eyes were glistening with wetness as she placed a sisterly kiss on his cheek.

"Don't worry Angelette, everything will work out fine," he reassured her, "we'll make sure the Germans don't hurt you again."

She stepped away and rubbed at her eyes. "Thank you. I go now, my papa probably needs me."

Angelette turned and walked away, disappearing round the side of the building without looking back. James watched her go, slid the photo back into his pocket, and made his way to his sleeping quarters where an odd smell hung in the air.

"Hey," Piper greeted him, tilting a glass jar in his direction. "These pickled onions are great, try one."

James contorted his fingers and just about managed to fish one out, grimacing as the sourness caused his taste buds to whither up and die. Piper roared with laughter.

"Here, there's cake and cheese as well. Some nice ladies dropped it off earlier."

James glanced out the window and saw David standing outside talking to Marie, Angelette's shy friend from the day before. Angelette herself popped into view a moment later but no-one else seemed to notice her as she traipsed off down the street by herself.

"Heard anything from the captain today?" James asked.

Piper shrugged and bit down on another onion without even flinching. "Dunno, not seen him."

David entered the room and nodded at James. "That Marie girl we bumped into yesterday," he began, a smile creeping across his face, "she speaks more English than she lets on y'know."

"Everyone speaks the language of love, Davey Boy," replied Piper, "especially the ladies."

A flicker of annoyance crossed David's face when he heard the nickname but the smile remained where it was. "They sure do."

Another soldier entered the room. "Hey, anyone seen the -" he began, before wrinkling up his nose in displeasure, "what's that bloody smell?"

Piper crunched down on another onion and made a sucking noise through the gap in his teeth. "Here, help yourself."

"Where'd you get all this food?" enquired the soldier.

David frowned. "Finders, keepers," he muttered around a freshly-lit cigarette.

A minute later James thought he heard something off in the distance and hushed everyone else into silence as a familiar droning sound buzzed around them.

"I reckon it's that German plane again," stated Piper. James nodded in agreement and moved towards the windows.

"There it is," he said, pointing at something in the sky. "And it's coming right towards us."

As the droning became louder and louder Smythe and two other soldiers walked into the room. The plane's wings tilted and the aircraft swooped down towards the ground, the rattle of machine gun fire cutting through the air like a knife.

"Trust us to be in the only part of France that doesn't have any anti-aircraft guns," someone complained.

"Nah, just ignore it and it'll go away," the captain announced, seeming to appear from nowhere.

James watched as the plane circled back up into the sky when an outrageous idea flared up inside his head. "It's only one plane," he reminded them, "I reckon we can shoot it down."

The captain snorted. "With what?"

"Does anyone here know how an anti-aircraft gun works?"

"Yeah," replied the captain, "you aim at the pilot and hope for the best."

"No," disagreed James, raising his voice to be heard over the sound of the approaching engines, "there's no such thing as a direct hit, it's all about filling the sky with clouds of shrapnel so the plane flies into it. Those shells explode into dozens of pieces, sending bits of metal flying in all directions."

Everyone in the room ducked instinctively as the plane roared down again, the sound of shattering glass and people screaming audible over the din of the machine guns.

"That's fascinating stuff, Professor," mocked the captain, "but so what?"

"So we can do the same thing with our guns and fill the air with bullets. We only need one lucky hit to take it down."

The captain looked indecisive and incredulous.

David's eyes narrowed as he looked at James. "I remember you trying something like this a few years ago."

The captain glanced at David and then back at James again. "Oh, Jesus Christ. Is this another load of Dunkirk nonsense? Because if it is, I really don't - "

David's face hardened as he wished he had kept his mouth shut whilst James felt a flash of anger run through him. "Look," he said through gritted teeth, "we can either stand here picking our noses or we can get out there and do something. How long do you think the people in this town are going to put up with us if they think we're as scared as they are?"

The captain once again looked indecisive.

"Right, I'm going out there to shoot that bastard down," James stated. He looked around, noting that everyone was looking at him, "Who's with me?"

There was a brief moment of silence that almost caused James to burst with fury until David spoke up first. "I'm in."

"Same," agreed Piper, "I didn't run all the way up that sodding beach just to sit here doing nothing."

Four more voices chimed in agreement and the sound of rifles being cocked and loaded was music to James' ears. "Follow me," he ordered.

"You're all mad," declared the captain as his squad filtered past him.

"Right," said James, stopping in the middle of the street and turning to face the others. "We need to put up a wall of bullets for that plane to fly into, so wait until I tell you to fire."

The aircraft was coming round for another strafing run, this time far lower than it had been before, the machine gunner blazing away at his leisure.

James raised his rifle, shouting to be heard above the roar of the engines. "Wait for my command! And aim just in front of it, it's coming in bloody fast!"

The plane rushed towards them, skimming the tops of trees and chimney pots like a bird of prey gliding over the surface of a lake, the engines filling the air and pulverising their ears with the din of a thousand lawnmowers charging towards them, hell bent on destroying everything in their path.

"Not yet!" James bellowed, the veins on his neck bulging against the strain. A cold sweat broke out across his entire body as a flicker of doubt washed over him, the sheer absurdity of what they were trying to do finally hitting home.

"Fire!" he shouted, his voice barely audible to those around him. Seven trigger fingers jerked and squeezed as rapidly as they could, filling the air in front of them with a curtain of long sharp bullets that could rip and tear through anything that tried to get in their way. As the rifles all bucked and jerked in the hands of their wielders, the roar of the plane drowned them out until they sounded like nothing more than a cluster of popped birthday balloons. A loud clanging explosion right above their heads made all seven of them duck instinctively and a heartbeat later the spluttering sound of a dead engine sent them into a delirious rapture as a trail of smoke started belching out from the left wing of the aircraft. James thrust his rifle into the air and roared like a wild animal, a thrill rushing through him as those around him followed his lead and did the exact same thing; the feeling of being in command, of facing the enemy and winning filling him with an overwhelming sense of power and righteousness. The plane tilted wildly and veered off to one side before disappearing behind a row of buildings and a few seconds later they all heard something large and metallic crunching and groaning as it flopped back down to earth.

Piper stood on his tiptoes, sniffing at the air as the acrid stench of burning fuel filled the street. "I don't know about anyone else but that smell of diesel is making me feel really horny."

Everyone, including David, roared with laughter, so much so that they didn't notice the captain rushing out of the building.

"We did it!" he exclaimed, without a hint of shame, "We shot those Jerry bastards right out of the sky!"

Several jaws were clenched in annoyance and a number of dirty looks were cast in the direction of the commanding officer, but he was utterly oblivious to them. A thin plume of smoke on the horizon was visible over the tops of the houses.

"Looks like it only crashed a mile or so away," stated Captain Jones, "we should go and take a look."

Still giddy with the thrill of victory, everyone assented to this order without any mutterings of protest.

"If we go round the back of our building we should be able to follow the smoke easily enough," James suggested, "it's all fields and woods that way."

"After you, then."

All eight of them eagerly set off in the direction of the crash site, pausing only to make sure their weapons were loaded and secured around their shoulders.

"Reckon we should take that axe?" David asked, pointing at the rusted tool that was pointing forlornly up at the sky, "Might need to use it to smash the side of the plane open."

"Don't be daft," scoffed the captain, "there's loads of us, the pilot will surrender the moment we knock on the door."

David's brow furrowed as he cast an angry look in the direction of the captain.

"Hang about, some of them aircrews are pretty big," one of the others pointed out, "how'd you know there's only one?"

"Fair point," agreed James, "might be a navigator, a gunner, a bombsight operator, or even -"

"Okay, bring the bloody axe then," the captain testily agreed.

David remained right where he was, pausing only to light himself a fresh cigarette. He had had an idea, had voiced that idea in good faith, only to have his input shot down and dismissed out of hand. As far as he was concerned that idea was dead and buried and he no longer had any interest in pursuing it... but if someone else wanted to take up his discarded mantle then they were free to do so.

"I'll grab it," one of them said, jogging over to the axe and pulling it free of the log.

They carried on walking in the direction of the smoke, passing by a large square of freshly dug up earth that reminded James of the vegetable patches that were now a regular feature of British gardens, as people supplemented their meagre food rations with anything they could get their hands on.

"Funny place to grow tomatoes," someone remarked.

"Nah," disagreed the captain, "them Nazis were stealing people's food so this is the ideal place to grow it in secret. Bet that forest is chock full of secret stashes."

A small light flickered in David's mind as he considered what else might be hidden amongst the trees. If the Nazis were stealing food, no doubt they would be looting valuables as well… and what self-respecting owner of valuables wouldn't want to sneak out at night and hide them somewhere safe?

As they neared the downed aircraft, James could see through the trees that it had landed awkwardly and its tail was sticking up in the air. "That's the same plane alright," he stated, pointing at the faded Swastika.

"Can we take a breather when we get there?" the axe carrier enquired, "It's further away than -"

A sudden burst of machine gun fire split the air and before David could react someone stumbled and fell against him.

"Get down!" James yelled, throwing himself to the ground and crawling towards a tree.

David rolled into a small dip and glanced back at the soldier who had fallen against him, only to find himself face to face with a young boy barely out of his teens, his throat little more than a mangled mess of flesh, blood gurgling from his mouth in fits and starts as he convulsed violently on the ground. The machine gun fire continued in loud bursts, showering them with leaves and broken branches as bullets tore through everything in their path. It stopped as suddenly as it began, leaving the seven of them to listen to the squelching gasps of their fallen comrade as his life rapidly drained away right before their eyes. David watched as the dying soldier jerked a final time, his body going limp, his eyes glazing over and turning into little more than lifeless marbles, his blood-soaked hand flopping down on the rusty axe that lay beside him. Although this wasn't the first time that David had seen someone die of horrendous injuries, he hadn't ever been surprised by it like this. One minute the soldier had been little more than a complaining young private who existed in the corner of his vision, and a rare feeling of guilt surged through David as he recalled his annoyance when he thought that the soldier had stumbled into him out of clumsiness.

There was a moment of silence as they all stared at the corpse. "Piper," said James, trying to control the anger in his voice, "see if you can take that German bastard out with that old girl of yours."

"With pleasure."

Piper flattened himself down on the grass and peered cautiously round the side of the tree he was using for cover. The machine gun remained silent and Piper slowly brought his rifle round in front of him, letting out a grunt as the roots of the tree dug into his chest, and peered through the scope. The aircraft leaped towards him, with every rivet and every dent and every scratch suddenly visible as if he were standing right next to it with a magnifying glass. Piper adjusted the angle and the tendrils of adrenaline tickled at his senses as he found himself looking into the glass dome at the top of the plane where the machine gunner was situated. A fist briefly appeared in front of the German's mouth and his head jerked as if he were coughing or sneezing. On the side of his face was a scar that looked too old to be a war wound yet could easily have been from a fight in a bar somewhere or perhaps even the result of being slapped by a woman's jewelled hand. Another burst of adrenaline surged through Piper as his world narrowed and shrank itself down to a single objective, a single moment where nothing else mattered, his lungs expanding and contracting in short bursts, his heart becoming an untamed and disruptive pendulum inside his chest as time slowed down to a crawl. The German blinked at the exact moment that Piper pulled the trigger, indelibly imprinting into his subconscious the illusion that he had killed a defenceless man in his sleep.

"Got him," Piper stated, his voice sounding dry and hoarse. He blinked a few times, feeling as if he had just emerged from a darkened room.

"Good," said James. "I doubt if they'll be popping their heads up again but we should stay low anyway."

They took a long detour around the side of the aircraft, using trees and bushes for cover, all of them keeping a wary eye on the bubble so as not to be taken by surprise again. As they approached the aircraft itself, the gruesome sight of a half-destroyed face pressed up against the blood stained glass stared morosely down at them.

"You got him good," stated the captain, but Piper chose to remain silent in spite of the compliment.

The door on the side of the plane had broken clean off, leading David to conclude that it would be easiest to just chuck a couple of grenades inside and be done with it.

"Smith," ordered the captain, "tell them to surrender or something."

Smythe barked a few words that were incomprehensible to everyone else yet there was no reply from within the aircraft. After a few moments he repeated himself, as did the resulting silence.

James bent down and picked up a fist sized stone. "This'll liven them up a bit," he said, tossing it into the plane. As it clattered around inside the aircraft, the unmistakeable sound of panic-stricken men trying to get out of harm's way could be heard.

"Yeah," confirmed Smythe, "that livened them up alright." After repeating his demand for the Germans to surrender he received a swift and eager reply. "They're coming out and they say they're unarmed."

There was more noise from inside the aircraft and the seven remaining British soldiers anxiously waited for the occupants to show themselves. A set of fingers appeared around the edge of the doorway and the first German to emerge was greeted with the sight of seven weapons pointing right at him. Smythe barked something prompting the German to lower himself down to the ground, his face etched with worry and concern. A few seconds later a second man appeared and Smythe repeated his instructions.

"Is this it? That's all of them?" James asked.

Smythe once again said something in German to the two men and when the taller one answered, James' finger itched to shoot him like he would a rabid dog.

"Which one's the pilot?" James enquired for no particular reason. When the taller German answered Smythe's question, James' compulsion to shoot him intensified for a moment.

"Alright, let's get them back to town," ordered the captain, "we can bung them in a cell until high command catch up with us."

The two prisoners were shoved towards the front where everyone could see them as they headed back. David cast a lingering look back at the downed plane, curious about what might be hidden away inside.

A smile appeared on James' face when he glanced back at the aircraft as he remembered an unforgettable moment from the year before. He had been rudely awoken by a soft pair of hands stroking and caressing him under the covers, something that brought him up from the depths of sleepy unconsciousness very quickly.

"Happy birthday, James," Mary had purred into his ear before climbing on top of him.

With that first treat out of the way, James disappeared into the bathroom for a nice hot bath.

"Don't spend too long in there," Mary called through the locked door, "we've got a whole day ahead of us yet!" she added cryptically.

There was an element of teasing in her voice and although it was impossible for him to know for sure, James couldn't shake the feeling that there had been a big smile on her face. After giving himself a suitable soaping down he dried himself off, got dressed, and went downstairs where he was welcomed by the tantalising smell of fried food.

"Ah, just in time!" Mary chimed, ushering him into the dining room, "Sit down and I'll bring it in."

A few minutes later a plate of fried sausages, bacon, eggs, sliced potatoes, and mushrooms was placed in front of him. Fresh orange juice and coffee seemed to appear from nowhere, prompting James to wonder if the war had suddenly ended and rationing was no longer in effect.

"Where…?" he wondered aloud.

Mary let out a small laugh. "If that butcher down the road didn't know about me before, he certainly does now. I've been pestering him every day for the past two weeks; the silly sod finally buckled when I went in wearing my uniform."

The two of them took full advantage of this rare feast as they quickly and gladly polished it all off. When everything was washed and packed away, Mary placed a kiss on his cheek.

"Okay, birthday boy, the day's not over yet. You'll need to go and put your uniform on though," she told him, a coy smile inching across her face, "less chance of us getting arrested that way."

As James went off to get changed, Mary had a quick bath herself and reappeared wearing her own uniform.

"Come on, then," she told him with a twinkle in her eye, "I borrowed one of the big trucks for today. I figured that if we look official there's less chance of us getting arrested."

James laughed and followed her outside to where an army supply lorry was parked and when he climbed up into the cab, he marvelled at how high up he was compared to all the other drivers on the road.

"Now then," Mary began, producing a scarf from her handbag, "this is a surprise so you'll have to put on this blindfold."

"Looks a bit suspicious," he observed, "what if it gets us arrested?"

"Then you'll just have to shoot your way out."

James put the blindfold on and turned to face her. "Are you making faces at me?"

"Of *course* not, darling," she answered in saccharine sweet voice, "I wouldn't do that to you on your birthday."

The vehicle roared into life and James settled himself in for the mystery journey, doing his best to make educated guesses about where they were going but soon found himself dozing off.

"Alright, you can take the blindfold off now," Mary told him sometime later, bringing them to a halt.

James took off the scarf and sat there blinking as his eyes struggled with the sudden brightness. Mary was sitting there looking at him with a tender smile on her face, one that held no hint of the strings she had to pull, nor the favours she had to call in, to arrange this day out.

"Is this… an airfield?" he asked, his voice suddenly full of childish wonder.

"Well spotted. Wait here while I find out who's entertaining us today," Mary answered, getting out of the truck and disappearing into a nearby building.

James glanced around, running his eyes up and down the long tarmac runway that seemed to stretch from one end of the world to the other. A number of large hangars were visible and another wave of boyish happiness washed over him as he fantasised about walking amongst an entire squadron of Spitfire airplanes.

"Come on," Mary called, reappearing from nowhere and breaking him out of his daydream, "time for some fun."

He clambered down from the truck and saw that there was an element of nervous tension in her face. "You alright?" he asked, putting his arm around her shoulder.

She nodded and smiled, putting her own arm around his waist. "I've never done this before so I'm going to be holding on tightly."

The two of them walked around the main building and off in the distance James spotted a tiny figure standing next to a large aircraft.

"Ah, that'll be our guide," Mary explained.

As they approached the end of the runway, James squinted as the tiny figure gradually came into view and he realised that this guide in scruffy overalls was actually a woman. He cast a curious glance down at Mary who seemed stiff and nervous, so he gave her hand a comforting squeeze.

"Mary!" the woman called as they approached her, "Good to see you again."

The two ladies embraced and James frowned as he realised that he recognised this other woman from somewhere.

"Ah, so you're the birthday boy," she smiled, extending her hand towards him, "I'm Maureen and I'm going to be your pilot for today."

James' mouth dropped open in surprise and he glanced from the pilot, to the plane, to Mary, and back to the pilot again… whereupon he suddenly remembered where he knew her from.

"Maureen…" he began, clicking his fingers and searching around in the depths of his memory for her surname, "Maureen *Dunlop?*"

"Um, yes," she answered, looking a little embarrassed.

James stared at her feeling like he had just been introduced to a celebrity as he thought back to how this girl's photo was pinned up inside several of the men's lockers back in his barracks.

"Your photo was all over the newspapers not too long ago, right? You looked great," he told her, just about managing to catch himself before he blurted out anything more.

Maureen laughed and turned a slight shade of red. "Oh, those blasted photographers get everywhere. I had people staring at me in the street for days afterwards."

James looked up at the immense towering form of the plane in front of them. "This is a Lancaster bomber, right?"

"Yes, that's right."

James looked down at her, not quite able to believe that this diminutive figure could pilot such an immense and powerful machine. "And you can fly these things?"

A frown briefly appeared on Maureen's face, one that suggested this wasn't the first time a man had taken it upon himself to question her ability as a pilot. "Yes, although sometimes I have trouble reaching the pedals."

It took James a heartbeat to realise that she was only joking. "Mind if I take a quick look around first? I've never been this close to one before."

"Be my guest."

James walked under the wing of the aircraft and gazed up at it in wonder, marvelling at all the flaps, folds, and bolts that simply weren't visible in any of the photos or newsreels he had pored over since the start of the war. He stood next to one of the wheels, finding himself fascinated that it was almost as tall as he was, before pressing his thumb into it as if he were checking his bicycle for a puncture. The rear of the plane was lower than the front and he ran his hand along the underside to try and get an understanding of the immense power behind such a behemoth. With these pre-flight checks over and done with he walked back to the two girls who smiled at him.

"Big old girl isn't she?" stated Maureen, "Ready to take her for a ride?"

James nodded, feeling as if he were in some kind of dream. "Yeah. Yeah, let's go."

As Maureen led the way up the steps, James could see that Mary was looking nervous again. "It'll be fine when we get up there," he said, reassuring her with a squeeze on the arm.

The interior of the plane reminded James of a cramped holiday caravan he had once stayed in, with everyone having to shuffle around each other and walk with a stoop so they didn't bang their heads on the low ceiling. Long lengths of wire crisscrossed along the walls, some of them disappearing behind large panels and emerging from the other side in a different colour. There was a curious smell of oil and metal that seemed to emanate from everything he looked at, almost as if the machine was sweating in anticipation of being set free from the confines of the runway.

"Here we go," said Maureen, settling herself into the pilot's seat in the cockpit. "James, you go in the middle and Mary can go next to you."

A thousand dials, knobs, and switches stared back at James as he set himself down and put on the headset that was handed to him. Mary sat down and let out a sigh, prompting James to give her hand another squeeze. Maureen produced a clipboard from down the side of her seat and made a quick note with a pencil. She glanced at a dial, made a note, pressed a button and made another note, before flicking three switches and putting the clipboard back. She reached forward and a smile appeared on her face as her finger hovered tantalisingly over a large red button.

"Hold on to your hats," she advised, a nugget of wisdom that turned out to be a huge understatement.

An immense sound startled James as the entire plane roared to life, the kind of sound that only a fearsome dragon could make as it prepared to lay waste to a town, when the whole world began to shake and vibrate as the engines kicked in and the huge propellers spun themselves up to an unimaginable speed. To his right Mary was looking palc and stiff in her smart uniform whilst to his left Maureen was as cool as a cucumber in her crumpled overalls.

"Going to bring her round first," Maureen explained, her voice sounding small and tinny through the headset.

James' eyes widened as the whirring and the roaring increased even further, something that seemed utterly impossible, and the world outside the cockpit began to shift and move. The noise and the vibration was so loud and so dominant that he couldn't actually feel the aircraft moving, it was like he had been dropped into the centre of a kaleidoscope and everything was being rotated around him. As the pilot flicked another switch James strained his ears as a strange muttering could be heard through his headset, until he realised that Maureen was humming leisurely as if her favourite song was being played on the radio. The world outside the cockpit continued to move and swirl around them until all that lay in front of them was a long expanse of tarmac that disappeared off into the distance. A tingle started somewhere in James' legs and ran up through his entire body as he tried to prepare himself for this journey into the unknown.

"Okay, boys and girls," Maureen cheerily announced, "this is when the fun really starts!"

The sound of the engines, of the propellers, of his seat, of the entire beast that he was sitting in intensified as the outside world began to rush past him, the runway zipping towards them and disappearing somewhere underneath the aircraft. The vibrations and the shaking became stronger and stronger until he thought that his veins were going to burst from his arms, and the trees that had been so far off in the distance were now bounding towards him, filling him with a nervousness that he had never experienced before. To his right Mary was sitting bolt upright, her face pale and clammy with fear, whilst to his left was Maureen in her baggy overalls, looking relaxed and happy, completely oblivious to everything around her, just another stupid girl who didn't know what she was doing. Why had he been so foolish to get inside this death machine with such a tiny, powerless person at the helm? Through the cockpit window James saw the trees vanish underneath him, leaving him looking at nothing but white fluffy clouds, and panic raced through him when the sensation that he was falling backwards threatened to overwhelm his mind.

"Allez-oop!" Maureen quipped as the aircraft left the ground.

There was a clunk from directly beneath them, leading James to wonder if the wings had fallen off.

"Don't worry, that's just the landing gear coming up."

After what felt like an eternity, the clouds shifted up and the pleasant green fields of England popped back into view as the plane levelled itself out again. When James looked at Mary again, he saw that her mouth was hanging open and a look of complete bewilderment was plastered across her face. She turned her head towards him, blinked twice, and smiled.

"We're... we're flying," she said, sounding utterly bewildered.

James looked back out of the cockpit, finally coming to terms with what was going on. "We're flying," he confirmed.

"Marvellous, isn't it?" Maureen stated, "Best feeling in the world."

"Can we stand up?" asked James.

Maureen let out a small chuckle. "You can dance the tango if you fancy giving it a go."

James stood up and peered out the window, watching in amazement as the world slowly slipped beneath them. He turned around and gestured for Mary to join him, who gingerly stood up and stared out at the beautiful view of the world they had.

"This is incredible," she said, sounding breathless.

"James, you can go and pop your head in the bubble if you want," said Maureen.

He shot her a quizzical look.

"The gunner's section. There's some stairs back there, they lead right down to it."

James removed his headset and made his way back through the aircraft, doing his best not to worry about somehow getting lost or falling through a trapdoor of some kind. He went down some steep steps and found himself standing in front of a large window that provided him with a bird's eye view of everything below them, giving him the impression that he was peering over the side of a flying carpet. He eased himself into the gunner's seat and spent a few moments getting used to moving the large machine gun around before squinting through the gun sight. James gazed down on endless rows of houses, buildings, and vehicles, realising just how powerless and defenceless those on the ground really were when being attacked from the sky. After a short while he made his way back up the stairs and returned to the cockpit to find that Mary had moved into his seat, her expression of panic and fear replaced with one of joy and exhilaration. When James sat down and put the headset back on, his ears were bombarded with the sound of two women laughing and chatting like old friends.

"What did I miss?" he asked.

Mary leaned over and planted a kiss on his cheek. "Nothing. Well, everything. This flying lark is the most amazing thing I've ever seen. You were right when you said it would be fine once we got up here."

James smiled back at her. "Don't worry, those big engines made me feel nervous as well."

The huge bank of dials, buttons, and switches caught his attention again and he tried to make sense of it all.

"What's that for?" he asked, pointing at a number that kept rotating round.

"That's our altitude," answered Maureen.

James nodded and pointed at another one.

"That's how fast we're going."

James stared at a third dial that didn't seem to be doing anything, doing his best to recall all the articles he had read about planes and how they work, before giving up and pestering the pilot for details.

She looked at him with a twinkle in her eye. "That's just a clock."

James laughed. "Can you do a barrel roll in this thing?"

"Nah, she's not really built for showing off. But hold on and let's see what we can do."

The world outside suddenly lurched to the right and a panic ran through James as his internal sense of balance started going haywire. He glanced at the pilot and the sight of her cheeky grin made him realise how foolish he was being. The plane began to level out, the nose once again resting firmly and safely on the horizon.

"Fancy a quick go, James?" Maureen asked.

"Really?" he asked with wide-eyed excitement, "Have a go at flying this plane?" Even though he was eager, he couldn't shake the notion that she was teasing him.

"Sure. Just grab that other wheel and move it to the left a tiny bit."

James reached out and placed his hands carefully around the wheel in front of him, not quite able to believe that a set of controls which looked more at home in a car would be capable of manoeuvring such a vast machine. Unable to shake the notion that he was going to send them plummeting to the ground, James' knuckles turned white as he twisted the wheel a bare fraction of an inch to the left.

"Oh, come on!" Maureen said with a chuckle, "Give it a bit more than that."

James turned the wheel some more and a thrill surged through him when he saw the horizon twitching and tilting in time with his wishes. He turned the wheel back to the centre, grinning as the ground below him evened out again. Feeling more emboldened he turned the wheel to right, once more feeling a surge of delight as the entire craft obeyed his simple command without so much as a groan, a sputter, or a protest.

"Marvellous, isn't it?" Maureen said, her voice full of earnestness.

James nodded in agreement, wondering why he hadn't joined the RAF instead of the army.

"So, fancy going anywhere in particular?" she casually enquired.

James' mouth dropped open as his mind rushed to explore the possibilities of such an open-ended question, one that kicked off a childhood memory of the first time he was given a bicycle of his own and a friend had asked him where they should go. He had stood there contemplating all the previously out of reach places that were suddenly within his grasp - the sweet shop down the road was no longer the long, tedious trip it used to be and the woods were now a place he could zip out to and then zip back from without having to worry about being home before it started to get dark… he could go *anywhere* he wanted to. Sitting there in the cockpit, his head buzzed and whirled with excitement as he considered the possibilities now available to him. What about Scotland? Wales? Ireland? Was there an airfield on the Isle of Wight? How about a quick trip to Paris to circle around the Eiffel Tower…?

"We could pop over to South Africa!" he blurted out, his imagination going into overdrive as he realised that the three of them could simply fly away and forget about the war. There would be no more air raids, no more rationing, no more suffering, and no more Germans. They could spend every day high amongst the clouds, searching for herds of wild beasts before coming down to land and setting off on a safari. He would propose to Mary and have a glorious wedding in the sweltering heat, go skinny dipping in immense lakes and swim through vast schools of colourful fish, gorge on tropical fruits, go camping, climb mountains, become a lion tamer, and build a luxurious castle in the middle of nowhere.

Maureen's face took on the surprised expression of someone who has just been told that they have won first prize in the local church raffle. "What? No, we… we can't," she replied, sounding as if she was saying something that she was struggling to believe herself. "We don't have enough fuel and we'd get shot down somewhere over France."

Reality bit down hard on James' hopes and for a brief moment, up there amongst the clouds with two of the most beautiful women he had ever met, he despised the Nazis more than he thought was possible. All too soon their time in the air came to an end and Maureen's face was full of regret as she turned the plane back round towards the airfield. Off in the distance the runway was little more than a grey pencil perched on a tiny piece of green felt and a sense of sadness filled James as it began swelling in size as they approached it. Mary reached over and slipped her hand into his, smiling at him in that girlishly vulnerable way again. There was a familiar *thunk* as the landing gear fell into place and soon the world was filled with greyness as the wheels touched back down onto the runway and they taxied safely off to one side. Maureen pulled out her clipboard again and repeated her earlier routine of noting something, flicking some switches, pressing a button, and making another note. The engines suddenly cut out, the propellers wound themselves down, and everything fell silent as if they were the last remaining people on the planet.

Maureen slumped back in her seat. "I hate that bit," she confessed, "it's like waking up in hospital and being told you're paralysed."

The three of them stood up and made their way back to the exit door, trudging down the metal steps like children who have been told that the rollercoaster is out of action. Once they were back on solid ground James stepped forward and hugged Maureen like a long-lost friend, lifting her clean off the ground and rocking her like a baby.

"That was amazing, I can't thank you enough."

Maureen laughed and flushed red. "It's Mary you should be thanking, she was the one who organised it."

James reached out and pulled Mary towards him, enveloping the two ladies in his arms and kissing them both on the forehead. "You two girls have given me the best birthday I've ever had."

"You're worth it," Mary told him.

James released them and looked back up at the Lancaster. "Have you ever flown a Spitfire?" he asked.

"Yes, many times," Maureen answered, speaking as if she had been asked if she liked strawberries and cream.

"What's it like?"

"It's almost impossible to describe," she answered, her face taking on a dreamy expression. "Those big bombers can be good fun but they're nothing compared to the Spitfires."

James looked at her expectantly, hoping for a fuller answer.

"With a Lancaster, it's like stepping into a giant elephant costume," she explained, "you can stomp around for a while but you can't do much more than fly in a straight line. A Spitfire... well, that's just something else."

Maureen paused and smiled, searching for the words. "It's like putting on a silk coat; it hardly weighs a thing and you can do whatever you want with it. You want to go left, the plane goes left. You want to do a loop and a twist, you do a loop and a twist. It's like being a fish in a pond, a quick flick of the tail and you're on the other side in a flash."

James looked at her with a mixture of awe and envy. "I'm going to buy Mary a silk coat for Christmas and borrow it whenever I can."

"You can buy me one as well if you like," laughed Maureen. "Well, do you two fancy staying for a cuppa?"

The three of them began the long walk back to the headquarters that doubled up as a canteen and general socialising area. After going in through the entrance, a large blackboard filled with timetables and flight schedules reminded James that this was a place of work rather than leisure, one that operated 24 hours a day just like his army barracks did. They went through a set of double doors and into a large room filled with tables and chairs and a small feeling of anxiety hit James when he realised the place was populated entirely by women, making him feel like an intruder. Over in one corner were three girls who had stripped down to their underwear to do some light aerobic exercises. One of them frowned at him for a moment but otherwise the trio just carried on with what they were doing. At another table was a woman darning her stockings, her head a blur of dazzling blonde hair and bright red lipstick.

"Are they real silk?" he asked.

The woman looked up and flashed him a confident smile. "You betcha!" she replied, surprising James with a strong New York accent.

As they continued through the room looking for an empty table, James noticed that the air was filled with exotic accents from all over the world. Maureen disappeared for a minute or so before returning with a tray of tea and buttered crumpets.

"Here we are," she said, placing it all on the table. "We usually have to make do with plain biscuits, so finish it off before any of this lot try to pinch it."

As he was the only man in the entire room, it wasn't long before a curious crowd had gathered around their table and James was soon fielding all kinds of questions about life in the army.

What countries have you been to? Do you get scared when fighting? How do you get washed and changed in your fox hole? Is there any heating in the barracks?

After a while James managed to turn the conversation around and began asking the women about their jobs. Although he had trouble understanding some of their accents, it soon became clear that despite the vast cultural differences between these pilots, they all had one thing in particular uniting them – a love of flying - and in some cases this passion had even saved their lives, with two Polish girls explaining how they had stolen an old biplane in order to escape Nazi occupation. Another had sailed all the way from Peru but was almost sent back due to speaking barely any English, whereas Maureen herself had been born and raised in Argentina.

"I came across with my sister," she explained. "My mother's English so we used to come here on holiday a lot anyway."

Shortly before it was time for James and Mary to go home, a small cake with a solitary candle was placed in the centre of the table and everyone gathered around to sing happy birthday.

"Honey, any time you fancy goin' flying again you get yourself back up here," called out a

111

particularly bold American girl. "Your handsome face is always welcome in my cockpit."

When he climbed back into the truck for the drive home, James caught sight of the discarded scarf lying on the floor. He picked it up and briefly considered putting it back on again - if he kept the journey to the airfield a secret, he could maintain the sensation that he had been transported to a magical place that could only be visited once.

Later that night, as they lay in bed, Mary let out a sad sigh. "James, you know when we were up in that plane and you said we should fly over to South Africa…?"

A pang of sadness ran through him as he recalled that moment of freedom. "Yeah."

"For a split second I really thought we were going to do it. I actually pictured us living in a big house, just you and me, riding on elephants and going on long safaris every day. Then we'd get back home and the servants would prepare a big feast for us. Can you imagine how much fun we could have?"

James smiled and stroked her face. "That'd be a dream come true. We should do it when the war is over."

"When the war is over," she agreed wistfully, "when the war is over."

A loud belch brought James back to reality.

"Them pickled onions are repeating on me," Piper complained.

The seven soldiers resumed their task of escorting their two prisoners back to the town, the air filled with the occasional outbreak of meaningless chatter. The two Germans wisely chose to remain silent.

"Hold on, I've got something in my shoe," stated Smythe, squatting down to untie his laces.

"Christ, your feet stink," Piper told him.

"True," agreed Smythe, squinting up into the bright sunlight. "How about I shove them up your backside when I get me boots back on?"

Laughter rippled through the group and some of them began throwing clumps of grass at Smythe as he tipped his shoe upside down to shake out a small stone.

"Find any gold in there?" asked Piper.

"Nah," answered Smythe, "just grated cheese."

Just as Smythe began worming his foot back into his boot, outrage and anger surged through James when he caught sight of the taller German pilot trying to sneak off whilst they were all distracted. He swung his rifle round with the quick and easy determination of someone closing a door on a disobedient dog, letting loose with two quick shots from the hip that sent the escapee tumbling to the floor.

Nein!

The other prisoner grabbed at his arm and James' anger boiled over into outright hatred and disgust. How can this pathetic and insignificant Nazi insect, a man that James had squared up to and defeated in the field of battle, think he is entitled to touch his conqueror? Instinct took over as years of bayonet training kicked in and James smashed the butt of his rifle hard across the German's face, before driving the barrel into his stomach. The German collapsed to the floor, writhing around in agony and spluttering as if someone had sliced his belly open.

"Touch me again you Kraut bastard," James snarled, his face bulging with fury, "and I'll shoot you with every bullet I've got!"

James stood over the fallen German, daring him to try anything again. In the ensuing silence, James' rage began to fade away as he stared down at the prostrate prisoner cowering in the grass.

"Grab the dead one and drag him back here, he might have useful documents on him," James ordered, turning back to the group.

Smythe and Piper walked over to the corpse, grabbed a foot each, and dragged it back to the group. As they began searching through his pockets, David bent down and relieved him of his watch with a quickness that suggested he had done it many times before.

"Finders, keepers," he quietly reminded everyone.

The remaining prisoner was hoisted to his feet and James winced when he saw how much blood was oozing from the fresh gash on his forehead. A distressed look appeared on the German's face when he realised that his fallen comrade was being looted and robbed as if he were nothing more than a dressmaker's mannequin. James found something on the horizon to look at when the German shot him a wary, fearful glance.

"Right, let's see if we can get Fritz here back in one piece," said the captain.

They set off at a faster pace than before and by the time they reached the outskirts of the town the German's face was saturated with his own blood.

"Look at that, Mr Nazi," one of the soldiers said, pointing at a half-collapsed house, "your friends did that."

A top window from across the street creaked open and a woman leaned out to shout at them.

Smythe let out a small laugh. "She seems to think we've captured Hitler himself."

As they moved through the town, more jeers and shouts were aimed in their general direction and it wasn't long before the emboldened residents started crowding around them. A rotten tomato whistled past David and landed at the feet of the captured airman. A moment later an egg splatted against his shoulder, much to the rapturous delight of the enlarged mob. A pretty blonde girl of no more than nineteen suddenly appeared, her face contorted with wild fury, screaming as she raked her nails across the prisoner's face.

Vous avez blesse papa!

James could see that the crowd was on the verge of surging forward and overwhelming them, yet their captain looked lost and confused. James raised his pistol into the air and fired it twice.

"Everyone get back!" he shouted, "This man is a prisoner of the British Army and is under our protection."

Smythe quickly translated this into French, prompting loud boos and jeers from the mob. James fired his pistol into the air again and stepped in front of the German just to make sure that nothing was lost in translation. Angelette glared at him before disappearing back into the crowd as the soldiers closed ranks and used their rifles to clear a way through the throng.

"Are they shouting at us or him?" James asked once they were free.

"A bit of both," answered Smythe.

"No more pickled onions for us," Piper lamented.

"Right, let's find the police station and get him locked up," ordered the captain. "Keep an eye out for any signposts."

Their journey lasted for another twenty minutes and was largely uneventful, save for the few people who decide to shout abuse at them from the safety of their own homes. Eventually they came to a large building with the word *Gendarmerie* written across the front.

"This'll be the place," advised Smythe.

The captain led the way and found himself in a gloomy, depressing room that served as the reception. Behind a desk was a man in an ill-fitting uniform idly smoking a cigarette and he looked up at his visitors with a bored expression on his face. His hair was thick, black, and slick, as was his moustache, and the cloak hanging over his shoulders reminded James of a Count Dracula film he had once seen in the cinema.

The captain cleared his throat. "We've got a German prisoner," he announced, "and he needs to go in a cell until we can hand him over to our, er, interrogators."

The man shrugged as if to say he hadn't understood a word that had been said, prompting Smythe to do the translation work again. The

Gendarme's expression tightened when he finally noticed the haggard-looking pilot in front of him. He stood up, walked round to the front of his desk, and slapped the prisoner hard across the cheek.

James grimaced as the German wailed pitifully. "Is there a doctor who can put a bandage on his wounds?"

When Smythe translated the question, the Frenchman's face hardened as he raised his hand to strike the prisoner a second time. A flash of annoyance ran through James and he caught hold of the Gendarme's arm before the blow landed.

"Leave it out," he demanded. The policeman glared defiantly at him for a moment before wrenching his arm free from James' grasp and muttered something under his breath.

"He says we can just leave him here," advised Smythe.

"I don't think that's a good idea, Sir," James said, addressing the captain. "We should escort him to wherever they're locking him up, just so they all know he's with us."

The Gendarme made no attempt to hide his annoyance at having his authority questioned, relenting only after much huffing and puffing, and swept his cloak back to make a show of the fact that he had a pistol attached to his side. The soldiers followed him down some steps and into another room that was even gloomier than the one they had just come from. A number of wooden doors stared silently back at them, the small barred windows offering a glimpse into the sheer amount of criminality that had been stored here over the years.

Two more Gendarmes were sitting behind another desk guarding the prisoners in a way that caused James to wonder if he had stepped into a medieval torture chamber. The three Frenchmen exchanged some words, none of which sounded particularly pleasant, and the two guards cast angry looks at the prisoner once they realised who he was. One of them stood up and opened a door, gesturing that this was the designated place for their guest of honour. When the door was slammed shut and locked, James peered in through the window and found himself almost feeling sorry for the German - his face was encrusted with clotting blood and his cheek looked as if it had been swiped by a wild animal.

"He needs a doctor," James said loudly, making sure that the hosts knew exactly what he was talking about. The three guards grumbled reluctantly but seemed to get the message.

"I thought my local bobby was bad," stated one of the soldiers when they were leaving, "but these belligerent Frenchies are something else."

"Is it worth leaving one of us behind, Sir?" James enquired half-heartedly.

"What for? It's not our job to babysit the French while they babysit the Germans. We're finished for now, let's just get back to our cosy little palace until the place calms down again."

***

Chapter Four

"Good news, gents," announced the captain a few hours later, "there's a show at the local church hall tonight and we're all invited."

"What sort of show?"

Captain Jones shrugged. "Dunno, singing and dancing I'd imagine."

"Fair enough. Do we have to get all dressed up for it?"

This time the captain rolled his eyes. "Those that're old enough can have a shave. You kids can just brush your hair or something."

The younger members of the squad exchanged annoyed looks but remained silent and the bathroom became a hive of activity as the men decided to make an effort to look presentable to the generous people of France. Sometime later later they were all standing outside waiting to set off again and James thought he caught a whiff of cheap aftershave when the captain eventually joined them.

"Everyone ready? Let's get going, I think I know the way," he told them, though the long meandering route they took towards the venue suggested he was as unsure of its location as the rest of them were.

"I can ask someone for directions if you like, Sir," offered Smythe.

"Don't be soft, lad. They'll think we're a bunch of idiots if we admit we can't even find a sodding church."

When they finally arrived a portly man welcomed them, making a point of shaking each of them by the hand. "Is good you have come!" he exclaimed, "We have special seats for you, please follow me."

James found himself surprised at how modern the building was. The exterior was rather bland and nondescript but once they got inside he saw that it made a nice change from the draughty old churches that were so common back in England. They were led to a hall that was crammed with chairs facing an empty stage, most of them filled with people waiting patiently for the show to start.

"Here, is for special guests," said the portly man, pointing to some seats on a raised platform, "mean you see over all else," he explained, making a show of standing on his tiptoes just to make sure they all knew what he meant.

Ten chairs had been set out for them and as the seven soldiers settled down and waited for the last few arrivals to take their seats, James felt a pang of sadness when he noticed that there were three empty spaces rather than just two. A few minutes later the lights began to dim, signifying that things were about to start, and as darkness claimed the room James noticed an attractive blonde girl push a wheelchair into the hall and take a seat near the back. A perfectly round circle of light appeared on the stage, revealing a smartly dressed man sitting on a stool. He raised his right hand and addressed the crowd.

Bonjour!

The entire hall was suddenly alive as every civilian, along with Smythe, returned the greeting. The man on the stool began speaking and gesturing with his hands, something that generated loud laughter from the audience.

"That's great!" applauded Smythe, turning to his neighbours, "Napoleon hated the Belgians as well, so…" he stopped when he realised that there was little chance of being able to explain the joke.

The man on the stage spoke for another minute or so, emitting more laughter from Smythe and the crowd, when a bright flame flickered to James' left as David lit himself a cigarette. The show lasted for just over an hour with the entertainment being something of a mixed bag for those that didn't speak French. A choir provided a dozen mouths singing a very pleasant, if somewhat perplexing, song while a solo female singer in a revealing dress was appreciated in ways that might not have been originally intended. The highlight, however, was when two clowns appeared to give a completely silent but heavily slapstick comedy routine that had every person of every nationality howling with laughter and demanding an encore. There was a feeling of disappointment when the show finally ended.

As the lights came back on David glanced curiously around the room, having forgotten that they were inside what was supposed to be a religious building. With all the heroic knights and sinless angels staring down at him from the stained glass windows and proclamations of *Love thy neighbour* written across the walls, he had always felt like an intruder whenever he stepped inside places of worship. This particular French church, however, was nothing like that and the air was heavy with the reassuring aroma of smoked cigarettes. He watched as porters rushed around stacking all the chairs up into neat little piles before wheeling them out of the room on trolleys. Four men in white jackets began hauling instruments up onto the stage and to his delight a small partition was raised at the back of the hall to reveal a well-stocked bar.

"Why can't religion always be this much fun?" he wondered out loud, lighting himself another cigarette.

"Well, boys," announced the captain, rubbing his hands together, "when in Rome, do as the Romans do."

The seven of them made their way to the bar whereby they were pleased to discover that there was no shortage of people willing to buy them a drink or two. They tried to make conversation as best as they could but found themselves struggling to understand the broken English once the music started playing.

After a while James caught sight of Angelette sitting next to an old man in a wheelchair. He watched her for about a minute, unsure of whether she would still be interested in his company, when she looked up and waved at him.

"She looks lonely," David told him, "why don't you go and cheer her up?"

As a matter of fact, James thought that she *did* look lonely but not in the suggestive way that David was implying – he couldn't shake the feeling that Angelette was used to being on her own and decided to go and speak to her.

"Hello, James," she said, sounding slightly unsure of herself. "You enjoy show?"

"I did!" he answered truthfully. "Those clowns… I've never seen anything like them before."

Angelette's face brightened. "Ah, they always very popular! They go touring around Paris sometimes but they originally from here."

The man in the wheelchair said something that James didn't understand.

"Oh, sorry," she apologised, "this is my papa."

James shook her father's hand, blurted out an awkward *bon-jaw,* and found himself surprised at how firm the old man's grip was. There was another exchange between father and daughter, one that caused Angelette to flush a slight shade of red.

Papa, non!

"Papa fought in the last war and he say you look like good soldier," she explained. Her father said something again and Angelette rolled her eyes in exasperation. "He say soldiers make good husbands and good fathers, so he hope you find lady to take care of here in France," she translated, looking somewhat embarrassed.

James smiled as he noticed a twinkle in the old man's eye, one that suggested he was a keen matchmaker for his daughter. He sat up straight in his wheelchair and saluted James smartly, who himself straightened up and respectfully returned the salute. Father and daughter chuckled as they exchanged a few more words and shared a private joke. James glanced back across the hall and caught sight of one or two of his squad dancing with a group of girls; when he turned back to Angelette she was looking up at him hopefully.

"Fancy a dance?" he asked. Out the corner of his eye he saw the old man give him a small nod.

Angelette smiled bashfully. "Yes, that would be nice."

They took a few steps and joined the crowd of dancers already enjoying themselves in the middle of the floor. James found Angelette to be uncharacteristically shy, which was a marked change from how bold and forward she had been before. He took her hand and was pleased to discover that she was more than familiar with the basic moves and after a few minutes she seemed to loosen up.

"Are you mad at me?" she asked.

"No, why would I be?"

"For earlier, when I hit the German's face. You looked very angry."

"I wasn't angry at you, I was angry at everything. That crowd would've stomped all over us if I hadn't done anything," James paused before continuing, "we also lost a man, he got shot when we approached the plane."

Angelette's eyes widened. "That is horrible and sad. What was his name?"

"I don't know," he confessed after thinking for a moment, "but he was only a young boy."

"That plane, it did so much damage to us. Yet it only had one man inside?"

"No, there were three of them. We shot the other two."

Angelette stopped and looked at him. "Really? Just like that, you killed them?"

"One was shooting at us, so we had no choice. The other one I shot when he tried to escape." Stating

124

what he had done out loud in such simple terms made him feel like a thoughtless criminal.

"Is not your fault," she told him, "they would have done same to you."

Angelette moved in close to James and initiated the dancing again. The smell of her perfume was intoxicating and the pressure of her body against his was captivating, yet somehow the spell she previously held over him was broken and neutered, her boldness and confidence nowhere to be seen.

"What would Mary do?" she asked, "If she saw a German prisoner?"

James was surprised at the question and he suddenly felt a great deal of pity for this attractive girl who was trying to compare herself to someone that she had never even met.

"Honestly? She'd probably do the same thing that you did, but with a cricket bat."

This answer seemed to satisfy Angelette and she smiled up at him happily. The two of them carried on dancing for as long as the band remained playing and James looked across the room just in time to see David disappearing out of the door with Marie.

"Thank you, James. You are good dancer and I had fun tonight," she told him on the way out. Before they departed she hugged him and placed a kiss on his cheek, with her father saluting him a final time.

When he arrived back at his room, Piper was already there and he looked up at James curiously.

"Surprised to see you back here," he said, "way you were dancing with that girl, I thought you'd be moving in with her."

"Nah, not my type," James replied, not untruthfully.

Piper raised his eyebrows. "You spend all evening with a girl you don't like… what on earth do you do with the ones you *do* like?"

James laughed and tapped at his nose with his finger. "That's none of your business. Anyway, how come you didn't get lucky?"

Piper shrugged. "I'm more of a talker than a dancer," he answered cryptically.

After thrusting another log into the fire, Piper sat down on the floor. "What's the story with your mate here?"

James had to think for a moment about who he was referring to. "David? Nothing much, we joined up at the same time."

"He doesn't really say a lot does he?"

"Nope," James agreed, "but you'd want him on your side during a fight."

"The strong silent type?"

James thought for a moment. "No, I'm not sure how you'd describe him. If you're looking to buy some stolen jewellery, he's definitely your man. If you want a shoulder to cry on, you'd be better off writing a letter to your mother."

Piper nodded slowly. "What if my mother's dead?"

"You'd still get more sympathy from her than David could ever offer."

Piper snorted out a small laugh. "Fair enough. I've met all kinds of people in the army. There's no shortage of wannabe poets and singers sleeping in foxholes every night. Seems like a waste of talent."

"Most artists dream of touring the world and there's been plenty of that this year."

"Hitler was an artist."

They looked at each other for a moment, both of them wondering how the conversation had taken such a dramatic turn.

"I'm gonna get some sleep," yawned James.

"Go for it. I just fancy burning a few more logs before turning in."

James yawned again and watched as Piper thrust another two sticks into the flames, before stretching himself out on the floor and closing his eyes.

***

Chapter Five

"I don't care if you've got a hangover," the captain lectured unsympathetically the following morning, "we lost a man yesterday and we need to go and bury him before the local wildlife sniffs him out."

James wondered if 'local wildlife' also included any potential German and French looters but kept his thoughts to himself.

The captain glanced over the assembled group that had gathered outside the building. "Okay, so only five of us made it back last night. The other two either got lucky or got lost, so... hang on, here comes number six."

"Morning, gents," chimed David, grinning from ear to ear. "It's a fine day and the sun is shining brightly and France is quickly becoming my favourite place to stay."

"Enjoy yourself last night?" asked Smythe.

"I did," David confirmed. "Enjoyed myself this morning as well, had a nice hot bath and a delicious breakfast, before enjoying myself a third and final time."

James caught sight of a number of envious glances from the others and he wondered what David had enjoyed the most – a night of socialising with the locals or being able to boast about it the next morning.

"You'll be nice and fresh for today, then," the captain told him. "Come on, let's get moving."

After David cottoned on to where they were going his grin faded and the bubble of smugness quickly deflated. In contrast to the jubilation that had sped them along this same path the day before, no-one was in any particular hurry this time around and they stopped for a brief rest on the way. When the shape of the dead soldier first appeared in the distance David felt a small pang of sickness settle in his stomach. A crow flew down and cawed loudly as it landed beside the body, causing a phantom taste of fish and saltiness to creep up the back of his throat.

"Well, here we are," the captain noted, breaking the silence that had dominated the journey.

The six of them stood there, their faces etched with a reluctant uncertainty that suggested none of them wanted to be the first to touch anything. The eyes of the fallen soldier were blank and staring, his skin white and dry, the ground underneath him thick and dark. For David the worst thing about this gruesome spectacle was the rusty axe staring accusingly at him, reminding him why he preferred to keep his mouth shut and leave the ideas and planning to other people.

"I'll take the first shift digging if you want," he announced, partly out of guilt and partly because he didn't want to have to touch the body itself. The boy's fingers were wrapped protectively - or perhaps desperately - around the axe handle and anyone trying to remove it would be fighting an unpleasant battle against rigor mortis.

As James and Piper exchanged a quick look of surprise with each other, the captain gladly handed over his trench tool. "Go for it."

David took a few steps away from the body, rolled his sleeves up, and started digging. Half an hour later, perspiring and breathing heavily, he held the spade up in defeat. "I'm done, someone else can have a go."

James took his place, who in turn was relieved by Piper, and so on until the captain deemed the hole to be deep enough. "Come on, give me a hand," he announced, grabbing hold of the shoulders. Three of them dragged and lowered the corpse into the hole before kicking the axe in with him. Filling in the grave afterwards was an easy enough job that the captain did himself and the rest of them waited patiently for him to finish.

As James stood there watching the hole being filled in an unpleasant thought passed across his mind as the events of the past few days rushed back through his consciousness. He frowned and looked over at Piper, who was biting down on a tomato that had been in his pocket.

Funny place to grow tomatoes.

James' knees gave way and he sat down on the grass with a heavy thump. The *tink tink tink* noise of a spade being patted against lose earth sounded distant, almost like he was hearing it from the other side of a thick wall. He heard a voice speaking, one that mentioned him by name but seemed to be too far away to be talking directly to him.

You alright, James? You look like you've just seen a ghost.

***

"Corporal Bowden, I'm not too keen on wild goose chases," began the captain, placing his hands on his hips, "so could you tell us exactly why you've dragged us out to this big cabbage patch again?" he jabbed his left boot into the loose earth.

"It's not a cabbage patch and it's not a secret tomato patch either."

The captain rolled his eyes and took a step back, leaving two large boot prints in the soil. "So now you're a clairvoyant as well a professor?"

James looked round at everyone. "You've all been growing vegetables in your gardens back home, right? Then you'll know that this soil is far too stony for growing anything in. You'd get nothing but weeds and worms living in it."

There was a low murmur of acknowledgement and the captain raised his eyebrows. "Fair point. So what's it for?"

James took a deep breath. "This," he said, pointing down at his superior's feet, "is a grave."

There was a moment of stunned silence which was broken by the captain. "What?" he cried, his eyes bulging out of their sockets.

"It's a grave," repeated James. "The mayor told you that the Germans took a load of civilians for slave labour, yeah? Well, I reckon that after a couple of miles they got fed up with their hostages so they shot them and buried them here."

"Jesus Christ," muttered the captain, suddenly unsure of where to put his feet. He stumbled and tripped over his own boots before finally scrambling his way back to solid ground.

"Hold on, how come no-one in the town heard all the shooting?" asked Smythe, "surely someone would get nosey and come to take a look."

James shrugged. "They probably did hear it. But there's explosions and fighting going on all over the place, so half the town are too scared to even leave their houses."

The captain rubbed his dirty hands down the side of his legs. "What're we going to do?"

The rest of them looked at their ranking officer incredulously until James spoke for all of them. "We can't keep something like this to ourselves."

"Wait, hold on," the captain protested, "we don't even know if there really are any bodies buried here. We can't just march into town and announce that we've found a mass grave without confirming it."

James frowned. "I'm buggered if I'm going to dig up a load of corpses after spending half a day burying one. In a town of this size there'll be undertakers who can do that kind of thing. I say we speak to the mayor and let him deal with the logistics."

A look of relief appeared on the captain's face. "Yeah. Yeah, that's a good idea. Let's go speak to him now, this place is giving me the creeps."

The six of them marched back sombrely, stopping only when they reached their dilapidated headquarters.

"Smith, you come with me to the town hall to do the talking," ordered the Captain. "You too, Bowden. Rest of you can just wait 'til we get back."

After navigating their way to the mayor's office, the three of them stood in front of the most French-looking Frenchman that James had ever seen.

The captain thrust his thumb in the direction of the mayor. "Tell him," the captain blandly instructed Smythe.

Smythe swallowed nervously and began stammering out what they had found. Although James didn't understand a word of what was being said, he paid close attention to the mayor's face as it expressed a range of emotions that started with a puzzled frown, moved through to wide-eyed astonishment, before settling on a pale and shell-shocked expression of disbelief.

"What did he say?" whispered the captain, once again breaking the silence.

"Um, not too much," answered Smythe, "but we're going to have to show him where it is."

The captain winced as if he had been hoping that his involvement in the matter had come to an end. "Alright, but I ain't bloody walking there again."

There were a few more stilted exchanges in French, during which the mayor regained his composure as Smythe grew increasingly uncomfortable.

"Okay, he's going to sort some transport out. We can go back to our place and he'll pick us up once he's got things organised."

"Sounds good to me," said the captain, looking relieved.

The three of them left the mayor's office and made their way back to their makeshift home.

"How'd it go?" Piper asked James.

"Dunno, I couldn't understand a bloody word they were saying," he confessed, "but his face looked as if someone had told him that Jack the Ripper was going to be staying at his house for the week."

A grim smile appeared on Piper's face. "I just hope you're wrong about all this."

"So do I."

"Me too," echoed David, "but if you're right, I don't want to go anywhere near that place. I just want to get out of here and never come back again. You ever seen the remains of women and children being pulled out of bombed out houses? Back home there's entire roads I don't walk down anymore thanks to those bloody Nazi bombers. When we crossed that channel, we were supposed to have left all that stuff behind us."

James knew how rare it was for David to say anything like this, preferring as he did to keep his emotions and thoughts to himself.

"Dave, if you fancy chatting to anyone feel free to give me a nudge," offered Piper.

David jabbed a fresh cigarette into his mouth. "Thanks, but I'm fine," he replied, speaking in a tone that suggested the conversation was over and done with.

A while later, the noisy sound of an engine filled the air as a tractor with a large trailer came into view through the window. A few seconds later Captain Jones popped his head into the room.

"Right, they're here," he said. "Come on Bowden, if I've got to go with them then so can you."

James followed the captain outside where an uncomfortable looking Smythe was already waiting and speaking with the mayor. In the back of the trailer were two men with dour expressions on their

134

faces surrounded by a selection of digging tools. An unpleasant feeling ran through James when he spotted the pickaxe, an item that seemed wholly inappropriate for unearthing the bodies of civilians. Although the two workers moved aside to make room for the three soldiers, they didn't seem to have any interest in acknowledging their presence beyond that. The mayor climbed into the driver's seat and started the engine up.

"Not every day you get personally chauffeured around by royalty," James quipped in an attempt to lighten the mood. Smythe shot him a weak smile but the captain remained silent.

The tractor continued down the road before turning off down a dirt track and emerging out into the fields. Every so often the mayor turned around to check with his English passengers to make sure he was going the correct way.

"Any idea what they're saying?" James asked, referring to the two Frenchmen who were conversing quietly with each other.

"I've only caught snatches of their conversation but I think they're bitching about the war and all the unwanted visitors they keep getting."

"The Germans?"

Smythe shrugged. "Germans, yeah. Us as well, I think, for eating their food and sleeping with their women. They also reckon we're wasting their time."

The trailer turned sharply, forcing the five passengers to reach out and brace themselves against the side, and a second later the engine was shut off. After they disembarked the three Frenchmen stood at the edge of the large patch of earth muttering and gesticulating to one another for a minute or so. The two workers grabbed a spade each and tried to hand one to James.

"No, we're not here to do any digging," the captain announced loudly, shaking his head and wagging a finger at them. The Frenchman shot him a dirty look before returning back to where the mayor was standing.

James lay down on the grass and watched as they started digging delicately and carefully into the loose earth. As the minutes ticked by and the pile of dug-up earth gradually became larger, James began to wonder – not to mention pray – if he had made a huge mistake. A sudden startled cry dashed that hope and James looked up to see the three Frenchmen standing and pointing at something in the ground. He glanced at Smythe and quickly concluded that he didn't need to ask for a translation - the expression on his face spoke volumes. The mayor gestured for the soldiers to come over and James found himself staring down at an arm protruding out of the soil. The skin looked stretched and leathery and the fingertips had dried and receded to give the nails a ghoulish elongated appearance, yet it was clear that they had uncovered the body of a young woman. A feeling of revulsion ran through him as his eyes flicked across the edges of the grave, sending his mind into a flurry of calculations and guesses about how many other corpses were buried here. A hint of an unpleasant smell tickled James' nose and out the corner of his eye he caught sight of the mayor covering his mouth and nose with a handkerchief. From behind him he heard someone let out a small groan. James rubbed his eyes as he tried to fit things into some kind of context that made sense. It wasn't all that long ago that he had been standing on a cliff looking down at the aftermath of the Normandy beach landings, the sea overflowing with dead soldiers, the sand pockmarked with decimated corpses, providing a sobering sight that made him realise how lucky he had been to survive. But standing here in a picture-perfect area of the French countryside on the edge of what appeared to be a mass grave... this was different.

"What is this?" asked Smythe, struggling to put his feelings into words, "I mean, what... why? What for?"

"It's a massacre," was all James could respond with.

"It's an outrage," added the captain.

The three Frenchmen talked animatedly amongst themselves for a few minutes before shovelling dirt back over the arm, something that James was grateful for. One of them retrieved a large tarpaulin sheet from the trailer and hunted around for some stones to weigh it down with.

"They're going to come back tomorrow with more people," Smythe translated.

"Thank Christ for that," muttered the captain, speaking for all three of them.

The drive back was a sombre affair that took place in an unpleasant silence that magnified every uncomfortable bump and swerve the return journey threw at them. The mayor dropped off his three British passengers with a mournful wave and the two workers finally acknowledged them with brief nods.

James walked into his room and found David staring out the window with a cigarette in his mouth.

"What did you find?" he asked, blowing out a hesitant stream of smoke.

James shrugged, not sure how to answer such a simple question. "A grave. There could be dozens of people buried there."

David remained motionless and silent, leading James to assume that David didn't believe him. "You saw the size of the bloody thing! We walked right past it!"

"What we going to do?"

"Nothing," James told him, before correcting himself, "I mean, we aren't, but they're going back tomorrow to, y'know, finish the job. Dig them up, I mean." He found himself floundering for the words and glanced around the room. "Where's Piper?"

"Out babysitting."

James swore under his breath and looked out the window in search of some kind of solace, when an idea popped into his head. "Fancy going for a coffee?"

David seemed to perk up at this suggestion and he tossed the remains of his cigarette into the fireplace. "Yeah, can do."

The two of them walked out and started off in the direction of the coffee shop.

"The world's gone mad," James remarked.

"It went mad a long time ago," David replied, speaking from experience.

A minute later David caught sight of two young girls playing with a skipping rope in the front garden of a house; to his surprise, James turned left.

"I thought the cafe place was this way," he queried, pointing in the direction of the girls.

"Let's go this way, see what else there is."

David shrugged and didn't bother to argue. As far as he was concerned a free coffee in one establishment was just as good as a free coffee in another. However, his mood changed as they approached a familiar looking building with a familiar looking word written above the door.

Gendarmerie

"What are you doing?" he asked, looking at James suspiciously.

"Just checking on our prisoner," James answered, glancing at the sign to avoid making eye contact.

The man who dressed like Dracula looked up at them stiffly and frowned as James pointed at the stairs to explain where he wanted to go. He grunted and waved them on, leaving the two soldiers to make their way down by themselves. A surly face stared out at them from behind a small barred window in a cell to their left, the kind of face that David was more than familiar with, the sort of face that was accustomed to spending long periods of time in prison. James approached the cell that the pilot had been shoved into the day before and peered through the window. The German was lying across a wooden bench, his eyes closed and his expression relaxed in a way that suggested he was fast asleep. His face had been cleaned up and the top of his head was covered with a rudimentary blood stained bandage. The Luftwaffe uniform, no doubt a source of immense pride and professionalism at one point, was dirty, limp, and torn, with dark patches that looked to be a mixture of blood, sweat, and urine. All being told, the German looked as if he had been treated reasonably well by his French keepers.

"Open the cell," James demanded, turning to the French guard and using his hand to make an unlocking gesture.

The guard shrugged and did as he was asked. The key was thick and heavy and the sound of the tumblers being turned over echoed around the room, startling the prisoner awake. The German sat up and blinked at his visitors a few times, his cowed, wary expression reminding James of a pet rabbit he once owned as a child - every time the hutch door was opened the nervous animal would retreat away from his eager hands. James flexed and stretched his fingers, unsure of what he wanted to do and why he was here, content for now to simply stare down the prisoner as if daring him to do something. After a few moments he moved his hand to where his pistol was holstered when something suddenly clamped down hard on his wrist.

"Don't be stupid," David hissed at him.

James had almost forgotten that David was even there and he looked at him in surprise, not quite able to believe that he of all people was trying to tell him what to do. He tried to pull his arm free but the grip tightened even more.

"I said don't be so bloody stupid," David growled, his eyes widening in anger.

"What do you care? Why're you taking his side in all this?"

"I don't give a shit about that sodding Kraut but what do you think shooting him is going to do?"

"It's about justice."

"That's bollocks and you know it. Killing him will lead you along a path that you don't want to go down. Trust me on this, the only place it goes is down the shitter. You've got everything waiting for you when you go back home so don't throw it away trying to be a hero. What you going to tell Mary if you get discharged? You think she'll be happy if you get court martialled for shooting prisoners? Just look at him, he's scared shitless and his war is over. There's thousands more just like him and you aren't going to be able to kill them all yourself."

They stared at each other in silence, neither of them quite able to believe what the other was doing, until James slowly began to relax his hold on the pistol. When David finally released his vice-like grip on his arm, James glared at the German a final time before angrily leaving the cell and storming back upstairs. David looked down at the prisoner, noting that his forehead was beading with sweat. He reached into his pocket with the intention of offering him a cigarette but this flare of generosity died as quickly as it appeared. Instead, he nodded grudgingly and followed after James.

"He's all yours," David advised the guard on his way out, jerking a thumb behind him.

Outside, James was sitting down on the building steps looking dejected and maybe even a little bit ashamed of himself, and when David came out and joined him he found an interesting looking crack in the concrete to occupy himself with. After a few seconds there was the familiar sound of someone striking a match.

141

"Still fancy that coffee?" David asked conversationally.

The question surprised James and he remained staring down at his boots for a moment longer. He looked up at David, searching his face for any sign of disappointment or patronising pity but found nothing; it was if their disagreement had been over something as trivial as whether to have boiled eggs or scrambled eggs for lunch.

"Yeah, why not?" he answered, grabbing at the chance to put the last few minutes behind him. An old memory flashed across his mind, reminding him of the last time he had been so ashamed of himself. He had been standing on a station platform idly working his way through a newspaper as he waited for his train home to arrive.

"Excuse me, Mister," a voice interrupted him, "would you mind getting me a cuppa? I'd go meself, only them Girl Guides say it's only for soldiers in uniform."

James had been in the middle of a yawn and as he turned to face whoever had disturbed him, it transformed into a grimace of disgust. Staring up at him was a girl with curly brown hair and a simple blue dress that hung loose from her slight shoulders. Trying to guess her age was nigh-on impossible as one side of her face was hideously burnt and scarred, making her look like something from a horror film.

"I've just come off a long shift and I'm awful thirsty," she continued. "Don't worry about your bag, I can look after it while you're gone."

James stared at her, feeling completely dumbstruck. As she spoke the burnt side of her mouth was as stiff as two old twigs whilst her lips on the other side wriggled as freely as a fleeing snake. Although there was a tired and weary look in one of her eyes, the other was surrounded by angry red flesh that made her look reptilian.

The sound of a guard blowing his whistle elsewhere in the station snapped James out of his trance. "Er, sure. Whatever you want."

He glanced down at the large army backpack that was on the ground next to him, wondering if leaving it with a complete stranger was really a good idea, before realising that it probably weighed more than she did.

"Ah, cheers, Mister," she said, sounding genuinely relieved.

James nodded and made his way over to where the tea was being served up, unable to decide if he was acting out of kindness or fear. Two of the Guides looked at each other and giggled from behind their hands when they caught sight of him.

"Back for more, Corporal?" a third one enquired cheerily, straightening her uniform and patting her hair.

"Erm, yes. Can you do me two cups of tea this time? I've got, um, a friend who wants one as well."

"Of course," she beamed, turning to the big metal vat behind her.

Out the corner of his eye, James could see two of the other Guides staring at him. When he turned and smiled at them their faces flushed red as they quickly went back to hiding behind their hands again.

"There we go, Corporal," said the serving girl, placing two cups in front of him. "We've also got some biscuits if you and your friend want one." She reached behind her and opened a tin without waiting for him to answer, placing a biscuit on each saucer. "They're for our lunch but we don't mind sharing with brave soldiers like you."

"Are you going to be a sergeant?" asked one of the others.

"It's not up to me I'm afraid," he explained with a smile.

"Well, I think you'd make a *splendid* sergeant," she told him. Her earlier shyness seemed to have evaporated and she stepped towards him, touching the chevrons on his arms. "I think the extra stripes look lovely on a soldier's uniform," she beamed.

"Oh, yes! And all those medals you'll be wearing when you come back as well!" chimed another.

By now the three girls had surrounded him and began peppering him with questions. He remained with them for a couple of minutes, happy to satisfy their curiosity until he remembered that someone was waiting for him. He thanked the Guides for the biscuits and they beamed with pride when he told them that all the soldiers appreciated their contribution to the war effort. As he carried the two cups back, there was a split second where he didn't recognise who was sitting on his rucksack. The girl was sitting at an angle, allowing him to see that she was just a normal girl of about eighteen years old when a pulse of disgust ran through him as she turned to face him full on.

"Oh, thanks, Mister," she said, sounding genuinely grateful, "and a biscuit, too! I haven't eaten for hours y'know."

As if to prove just how hungry she was, the girl ate the biscuit in two quick bites and took a sip of her tea before smiling up at him again.

"What's your name?" he asked, doing his best to avoid staring at her.

"Me name's Nancy, though some call me Nan for short. I get called worse, o'course, but I just ignore it."

"Pleased to meet you, Nancy," he said, holding his hand out. He felt stiff and awkward, almost as if he were trying too hard to be friendly. "I'm James."

"Pleasure to be in your company, James. That's a nice name, that is, I like it a lot."

James blinked. "So, erm, what kind of things are you involved in?"

"Workin' in a factory makin' things for the war. Some weeks I'm makin' bombs, some weeks I'm makin' bullets," she paused for a moment, "it's how I got burnt, y'see."

"Burnt? Oh yeah, I barely noticed it at first," he replied, not quite sure who he was trying to convince.

She let out a small laugh. "That's very kind of you to say so, but I seen you staring. Everybody stares but I can't say I blame 'em."

"What happened?"

Nancy took a gulp of tea. "Was when I was working with the fabrics for all the uniforms. I really liked it at first, running me hands all over that lovely material. Sometimes I'd daydream about cutting meself off a strip to take home and make a new outfit with it. It was marvellous seeing all the bits go in one end of the machine and coming out the other end as a jacket. There was all kinds coming out and if you named it we probably made it. Army, navy, air force, the lot, and we'd hang 'em all up in a row afterwards to dry. There would be so many that it was almost like having our own troop of warriors looking over us to keep us safe. When it was quiet we'd think up names for them and when no-one was looking sometimes we'd write little notes and slip them into the pockets. Some of the saucier girls would even put down their home addresses, hoping that a handsome pilot would fly down and sweep 'em off their feet."

Nancy laughed and smiled as she remembered the good times.

"One day, a big tub of the acid we used to treat the cotton splashed up in my face. I don't really remember it exactly but afterwards they said I was screaming me head off and they had to keep me in hospital for a fortnight afterwards. When I looked in the mirror for the first time I wanted to lay down and die. It was really painful at first, especially when I started crying, but it's mostly okay now."

After listening to Nancy's story James couldn't help but feel sorry for her. He glanced down at his own uniform and wondered what sacrifices other factory girls like her might have had to endure in order to get it shunted along the assembly line.

"You can have my biscuit if you're still hungry," he said, handing it to her. A rush of embarrassment ran through him as he realised what a futile, piecemeal gesture it was.

She smiled and took it eagerly. "Sure, if you don't mind!"

"How long you been working at the factory?"

"Over a year now though they moved me away from the clothes 'cos it made me nervous. Shame really as I used to enjoy it so much. Makin' parts for bombs just ain't the same, 'specially with all them dangerous chemicals about the place. We can't take anything metal in with us in case it causes a spark and blows us all to Kingdom Come. One girl forgot the rules and got sacked 'cos she was wearing a hairpin. Them foremen have eyes like a hawk, ain't nothing that gets past 'em."

Nancy finished off her tea and curled her small hands around the cup before continuing.

"Still, I can't complain too much. The money is nice and I'm earning more than what me dad gets working down the mines. I ain't told him though, he'd go spare if he knew his little girl was bein' paid more than him. I count meself lucky compared to some. You boys all get called up and sent away, only to come back a month later with an arm or a leg missing. Some of 'em won't ever come back at all, dying out in the desert somewhere or going down with their ship out in the middle of the sea. We all has a job to do, just got to get on with it."

James looked down at her, feeling strangely in awe of this small girl who, a mere few minutes ago, had horrified him so spectacularly, and realised that compared to her he hadn't really suffered much personal loss at all.

"I lost a few friends at Dunkirk," he said, mindful of the fact that he himself had returned unscathed.

"Those Germans really didn't want us to get back home."

"I was down in Dover for that and saw the soldiers coming off the ships," she told him. "Some of their uniforms were so badly torn that they was almost naked and they all looked so tired and worn out. It was after seeing all those poor men that made me sign up for the factory work. I wanted to do my bit."

James drained his tea and took the two cups back to the tea station. When the three Guides waved at him cheerily, he felt a pang of annoyance towards them for ignoring the needs of people like Nancy. As he walked back to the platform his train was pulling into the station and he opened the carriage door for his new friend. After finding themselves some seats, Nancy asked if she could sit next to the window and it took James a moment to realise that she simply wanted to sit so that he could only see the good side of her face. A few minutes into the journey Nancy let out a small yawn and announced that she was tired. As her eyes began to droop, James caught sight of the sun shining through her eyelashes and he got an insight into how pretty she must have been before her accident. When the train called in at the next station James felt another pulse of annoyance as he spotted a group of school children pointing and laughing at Nancy's disfigured face through the window. He glared at them and silently shooed them away with his hand before gently putting his arm around her so she could sleep up against him. James experienced a moment of discomfort as he fought against the compulsion to stroke the scarred side of her face and he started wondering what other horrors the war had in store for either of them. No doubt Nancy's life was destined to be one of loneliness, with her circle of friends gradually shrinking down to nothing and the invitations to go dancing with the boys drying up almost entirely. But what of him? If an army general suffered a moment of madness and sent his men to certain death, what did society have in store for those who returned with missing arms and legs? Would people be making faces and laughing at him behind his back as he sat in his wheelchair? Would Mary be willing to look after someone who was permanently disabled? If something happened to Mary would *he* be willing to stay with someone who was permanently disabled? Would either of them be as accepting of their predicament as Nancy was about hers?

He looked down at her sleeping form and suddenly felt ashamed at how he had initially reacted to her deformed appearance. For a brief moment he considered inviting her back to his house for dinner, before realising that explaining the sudden appearance of a complete stranger at the dinner table to Mary was something he could do without. He debated whether it was worth apologising for staring at her scars, or perhaps whether he should give her some money, or ask if she wanted him to introduce her to some of his soldier friends... but realised that he'd only end up embarrassing the pair of them. The train began to slow down again and James saw that they were approaching his stop. Nancy woke up as he removed his arm, disappointment settling on her face when he said that it was time for him to leave.

"Was nice to meet ya, James. Good luck with the future, hopefully we'll see each other again."

He bent down and placed a kiss her on the forehead and stroked her good cheek. "I hope so, Nancy. All the best to you as well."

She smiled up at him a final time, her eyes shining brightly as both sides of her face seemed to glow in a way that could only be a blush. He opened the carriage door, stepped down onto the platform and looked back at her through the window. The sky was cloudy, creating a reflective glare on the glass that softened the appearance of her face, giving James a final glimpse as to how Nancy must have looked before her accident. He raised his hand to wave goodbye and they disappeared from each other's lives forever.

***

Chapter Six

Two days went by, both of which were low on drama but high in peculiarity for some of the British soldiers. James found it strange wandering around the town, watching the French civilians going about their lives, many of them waving at him and treating him like royalty, fully aware that unbeknownst to them some of their friends and family members were being exhumed. This knowledge, this awful secret, felt like a burden that was poisoning him from the inside as every missing roof tile looked like the start of an avalanche, every bit of discarded litter blowing down the street signalled the end of the world, and every shout or cry heard off in the distance made him wonder if the news had finally broken.

David knew that these free and easy days weren't going to last so he decided that waking up and having breakfast with Marie was the best use of this time. Although he was more than aware of what was going on just outside the town, the decisions about what was happening and when it was going to be made public had nothing to do with him so he had no real reason to concern himself with it.

Piper decided that the best way to forget about their grisly discovery was to carry on playing with the local children, and it was rare to see him without a small child hanging from his back or slipping a small hand into his pocket searching for whatever toys they thought soldiers carried around with them. The parents, especially the mothers, had developed a soft spot for this jovial, smiling soldier who spoke the language of children far better than he did the French language. Food, wine, beer, and freshly baked cakes from enchanted civilians began piling up in his room, leading him to have a picnic that adults, soldiers, and kids alike were invited to.

Partway through the second day, the sound of church bells surprised them all.

James looked at Smythe with a frown. "That's the first time I've heard any bells ringing since we got here."

"Maybe they've only just fixed the clanger," suggested Piper.

The bells continued ringing for what seemed like an extraordinary long time, a sound that dominated the entire town and made everyone feel as if they were the last remaining person on the planet.

"I counted well over twenty rings. What's that mean?" asked Smythe.

"Maybe French priests like to use the twenty four clock," quipped Piper.

"I think it means we've got a body count," replied James.

"Oh, bloody Christ."

Half an hour later they spotted someone putting notices up on lampposts and trees. James took one down and handed it to Smythe. "What's it say?"

Smythe looked at it for a few moments and grimaced. "Bloody hell, whoever wrote this has an eye for propaganda."

"That's journalists for you. The Germans probably kept them under tight control so now they're making up for lost time. What's it say?"

"Blah, blah, blah, announcement to be made later this evening, blah, blah, either at that town hall place or by radio for those that managed to keep them hidden away from the Nazis."

James shook his head and scrunched his face up. "Probably best if we give that a miss, they might be annoyed if they find out we've known all this time." He paused before justifying himself further with, "And I won't be able to understand a bloody word they're saying anyway."

Within the hour groups of people were gathering around the notices to speculate what it was all about. James watched them from the relative comfort of the dusty room that he shared with David and Piper, wondering what was going to happen next.

"Where they going to bury all the bodies again?" asked Smythe.

"Most of them will be cremated is my guess," answered James. "A few of the families might be able to afford burial plots but most won't."

"Good time to be an undertaker," added David, "they'll be crying crocodile tears over this in public and sending out the bills by first class post before the day is over."

James thought he detected an element of respect in David's voice, "When one bugger starts a war, another bugger will be making his fortune from it," he observed philosophically.

David nodded in agreement. He was more than familiar with the idea of profiting from war, having done it himself on many occasions. Sometimes, like when it came to selling guns to the highest bidder, they were direct, but some of the subtler benefits of being involved with the armed forces were the ones he was most fond of. David's unsavoury connections from his civilian life meant that he knew most of the bouncers and doormen who were left in charge of the entrances to bars and nightclubs, meaning he could walk right into high society establishments that others would have to queue for an hour or more outside. The free entry was a nice bonus too, as were the discounted prices he was charged for drinks by the bar staff when he lied about being an officer in the army.

One particular night he found himself talking to two women who had taken a liking to him. They were quite wealthy, or at least their husbands were, something that they weren't shy about showing off and past experience told him that if he exaggerated his voice to mimic that of an East London rogue these types of women would view him as a pleasant novelty. Some of them were genuinely attracted to him, especially after he told them an embellished anecdote or two, whilst others viewed him as a cute little pet who was fun to have around for a few hours; two situations that suited David fine.

At one point during the night the two women disappeared into the toilets, leaving David by himself as they dashed off to powder their noses. As he lit himself a fresh cigarette, a pulse of opportunistic adrenaline rushed through him when his eyes settled on the purse that had been left on the table. He took a deep drag on the cigarette, the nicotine mixing in with his rising excitement, before blowing out two smoke rings that dispersed and dissipated amongst the array of empty wine glasses in front of him. His eyes flicked quickly around the room, noting that in spite of how many people were present no-one was actually taking any notice of him at all. The door leading to the ladies' toilet was just about visible and he could see that it was closed, with no sign of either of the two women making their way back through the maze of tables towards him. David slowly slid his arm between the wine glasses and the ash trays and flicked the purse open with an ease that suggested he had done it many times before, revealing a roll of cash and one or two items of jewellery. He swept his eyes across the room again, taking in every face that might be looking in his direction, searching for that one potential witness who might remember seeing a man with his fingers inside a woman's purse. The door to the toilet was still closed. The seconds were ticking by, the queue at the bar was getting deeper, the sound of people laughing, talking, and flirting was getting louder, and the door to the toilet was *still* closed.

Somewhere on the other side of the room there was the sound of breaking glass, as clear an indication as any that the night was getting into full swing. Dozens of heads turned towards the noise and rounds of ironic applause broke out sporadically amongst the revellers as they congratulated whomever had let the alcohol upset their hold on their drink. David squashed out his cigarette in the ashtray and snatched up the purse with the same hand in a smooth, well-practiced movement and walked quickly and briskly to the exit whilst everyone was still distracted. The purse remained firmly in his pocket until he got back home after which he emptied it out onto the kitchen table to count out his winnings. The cash, whilst not a particularly significant amount for someone with a wealthy spouse, was a considerable sum for anyone having to make do on a mere private's wage. Finding out the value of the jewellery took over a week due to him having to get in touch with other people, whereupon he discovered that the necklace was practically worthless due to it being nothing more than a cheap gold coloured piece of scrap. Although this was something of an annoyance to David, to a certain degree it was probably just as well: stolen cash was virtually impossible to trace whereas expensive personal effects have a tendency to leave a trail that can be followed if the original owner is persistent enough.

A loud crunching noise filled the air. "These French apples ain't half bad y'know," remarked Piper, his left cheek bulging like a hamster's pouch, "not as tasty at the trusty old Granny Smith but they've definitely got their own unique charm."

"Your taste buds must be shot to pieces. Do you like anything sweet?" asked Smythe.

Piper shrugged and thought for a moment. "Does liquorice and aniseed count?"

"I bet it's you who's been stinking the toilet out each day."

"Yeah," he confirmed, grinning like a mischievous monkey, "it's me who leaves all them dirty marks in the pan as well."

"Filthy sod."

Soon afterwards someone produced a battered pack of playing cards. Initially they played for matchsticks but it wasn't long before the more competitive players insisted on gambling for cigarettes. After a good start that had him smiling like a Cheshire cat, David's mood began sinking as his fortunes were reversed and his well-maintained supply of tobacco began to dwindle until he was forced to quit altogether. It was now starting to get dark outside and he turned his attention to the stack of wood in the corner of the room, staring morosely into the cold fireplace as he got an unshakeable feeling that the good times were almost over.

***

Chapter Seven

"Tell you what," said Piper as they walked back from the coffee shop, "the French certainly know how to mix up a decent coffee."

"It also used to be free," remarked David.

"Well, yeah, I guess things have changed a bit now."

"Has it?" asked James, looking around, "hardly anything has changed, the place is no different to what it was yesterday."

"What were you expecting?"

"No idea to be honest. Just thought people would be angry and out on the streets."

"Nah," disagreed Piper, "they've had several odd years of Nazi occupation, it's taken the fight right out of them. All their grief and anguish will be done indoors, it's why we've barely seen a soul today."

"My French teacher always went on about how fiery the French were. She reckoned they didn't put up with any nonsense from anyone," claimed Smythe.

"Yeah she was right but about two thousand years out of date. They ran out of steam after fighting Julius Caesar for so long," Piper told him.

"What about Napoleon? He was French and he took on half of Europe."

"True," Piper acknowledged, "but then the Duke of Wellington hopped over on a boat and started showing him how the game of soldiers is supposed to be played."

"Hang about, didn't the French declare war on Germany before we did back in 1914?"

Piper looked at Smythe with a wry smile. "Did you have a crush on this teacher of yours? You seem to have swallowed everything she told you."

Smythe laughed and turned a slight shade of red.

Just as their makeshift home appeared on the horizon they were accosted by the sound of three British military trucks driving up behind them. The lead vehicle slowed down and stopped in the middle of the road.

"Alright, chaps?" the man in the passenger seat jovially greeted them. He wound his window down the last few inches and leaned out, revealing three pips on his uniform that indicated he was a captain. "How long have you lot been here?"

There was a moment of silence before James spoke up. "We've been here just under a week."

"Really?" the man asked, sounding surprised. "How many of you?"

"Seven," stated James, before adding, "though there were eight of us originally."

The officer winced. "Sorry to hear that, chaps. What you been up to?"

"Not much," James answered modestly, "Captain Jones brought us here to check the place out and we lost a man bagging ourselves a Nazi prisoner. Oh, and it turns out that the Germans shot a load of civilians and buried them a couple of miles outside town."

The man let out a whistle. "No wonder they all look so miserable in this place. Good work though, chaps." He leaned back into the truck as if he was preparing to drive off again, when he paused and looked down at James again. "Hold on, did you say Captain Jones? As in, *the* Captain Jones...?"

James shrugged.

"If it's the one I'm thinking about, he's a complete wanker. What's he look like?"

"Bit shorter than me, curly dark hair," James answered.

The man rolled his eyes. "That sounds like him. Silly wanker is bloody useless."

"He told us he served in North Africa."

"That's 'cos he's a wanker. Top brass only sent him over there because he's such a pain in the arse. Everyone had bets on how long it would be before he got lost in the desert or eaten by a crocodile."

The four of them snorted with laughter and a grin spread across the officer's face

"I'm Captain Spark by the way," he told them, squinting at something in the distance, "is that your Captain Jones down there?"

James could see a figure in uniform standing outside their makeshift HQ, someone who may or may not have been Jones. "Might be, can't really tell from here."

"Oh, I can; I'd spot the soppy bastard a mile off," claimed Spark. He cupped his hands around his mouth and bellowed at the top of his voice "Oy, wanker!"

Spark shook his head. "You know them film clips that did the rounds a while back, of the Desert Rats frying eggs on the outside of their tanks? Don't ask me how, but that bugger is in one of them. Couldn't believe it when I saw his mug pop up on the cinema screen."

"Some people get all the luck," remarked Piper.

"Yeah, especially if they're a wanker," agreed Spark. A frown appeared on his face. "Can anyone else smell pickled onions? I've taken a real fancy to them since arriving here, the French hand them out like sweets."

Piper grinned and produced a small jar from his pocket. "Help y'self, Sir."

Spark's eyes lit up and he reached gladly into the offered jar, helping himself to as many as the narrow glass would allow his fingers to grab hold of. "Soldier, you're an absolute angel." He popped two into his mouth and crunched down on them. "I tell you something, next bit of home leave I get I'm taking a dozen jars of these back to the wife. She probably won't like them but she'll happy to make me some more."

"She won't like your smelly arse though," Piper advised.

"Nah, I'll just blame it on the dog," Spark deadpanned. "By the way, do any of you lot speak French?"

"I do, Sir," answered Smythe.

"Nice one, chap," replied Spark, crunching down on the last onion. "If you bump into any French chefs, could you ask them for the recipe for these things? It'll make a nice change if I can send something cultured back with my letters home."

"So what's the plan, Sir?" asked James. "We all moving out?"

"Nah, quite the opposite I'm afraid. The boys in intelligence are telling us that the Germans are on their way and we've been tasked with shoving some guns in their face. Got half a battalion backing us up that should be arriving soon, tanks and all." He paused for a moment. "Rumour has it that the Yanks might be lending us a hand but I'll believe it when I see it."

The four soldiers exchanged a glance with each other and Spark shot them a knowing wink.

"Holiday's over I'm afraid, chaps, so get your girlfriends to wash your underpants so you're all nice and clean for Jerry when he gets here." He pointed at the building in the distance which now had two uniformed men standing outside it. "That where you're all camped?"

James nodded.

"That'll be our first stop then. Hop on in the back of the truck if there's room, no point using your legs when there's friendly wheels about."

James led the way round the back of the vehicle and pulled himself up into it. A collection of faces stared back at him, some of them so young and fresh that they looked as if they were new recruits fresh from training, whilst a number of others had the grizzled and hollow-eyed look of D-Day veterans who would never forget their journey up the beach. Heads bobbed up and down and boots shuffled across the floor as the men shifted along the benches to make room for the newcomers. Some of them acknowledged James with a quick nod whereas others paid him little attention. The truck remained stationary for a further minute, during which Piper shared out the remains of his jar of onions. David lit up a fresh cigarette and twirled his lighter around in his hands, preferring to stay silent, leaving Smythe to fight a losing battle to make himself comfortable on the small corner of the seat he had been left with. The truck lurched forward with an awkward grind of gears and the air was filled with the tuts and curses of annoyed men.

"Sodding driver, he stalls the engine every time he changes gear. I swear he's driven us over every blasted pothole in France," one of them complained.

James smiled to himself and thought back to the early days of his relationship with Mary. The moment she found out that he didn't have a driver's license, she pestered him into letting her teach him and it wasn't long before she was bringing home all kinds of cars, trucks, and lorries just so she could drag him into the driver's seat. In return James taught her how to remove a punctured tyre from a bicycle using a penny coin and, after lots of coaxing and encouragement, how to disassemble and clean a pistol. The pistol was actually a German Luger, the one and only souvenir he had brought back with him from Dunkirk. Its original owner had been a German soldier who had crept up on him during a night patrol and it was only due to some quick-thinking from David that he had come out of it alive. In fact it was David who had retrieved the pistol for him in the first place.

Mary had initially turned her nose up at the thought of going anywhere near the Luger, stating that she had no desire to touch any nasty German contraptions of death. James' persistence eventually paid off and once she had seen it taken apart and laid out on their kitchen table, Mary found that she was no longer intimidated by it. She even developed something of a hobby for herself, seeing how quickly she could dismantle the pistol and put it back to together again.

"The enemy isn't so frightening when you've dismantled his weapons and placed all the bits next to a vase of flowers," James overheard her explaining to a friend, "I'm more likely to get hurt cutting up a cheese sandwich."

The drive back to their headquarters was a short but surprisingly bumpy one, lending credence to the earlier accusation that the driver really was going over every pothole in the country. When James hopped out the back of the truck he noticed that Captain Jones was standing there looking rather uneasy. Spark stepped down from the front and made a beeline for Jones without even bothering to shut his door.

"Good to see you're alive and well, Jonesy," he announced with a small hint of sarcasm.

"Yes, it is," Jones replied flatly. "What're you doing here?"

"Well, there's a war on you know," Spark reminded him, "and it's coming right this way. Major Andrews has tasked me with getting things organised until he arrives. Shall we step into your office so we can catch up?"

Jones nodded and headed back into the building. Spark turned around and instructed his men to get out and stretch their legs, only to discover that most of them were already milling around and stamping the stiffness from their feet. Within the space of a few minutes the presence of three badly-parked trucks and two dozen men had caused a traffic jam as cars, horse drawn carts, and bicycles alike struggled to move along the crowded road, a situation that was only relieved when James pointed out to one of the sergeants that it would be better if they all moved round to the back of the building.

"Hey, look at all them logs," one of them remarked, "if we had an axe we could get a nice campfire going."

When the two captains re-emerged, they announced their intention to go and speak to the mayor.

"Smythe, we'll need your French talents for this," explained Spark. "Rest of you chaps behave yourselves, I don't want any complaints from the ladies because you've been trying to look up their skirts."

The three of them hopped into a truck and narrowly avoided knocking a man off his bike as they sped off down the road. James went into his room and found David busy making sure that his supply of cigarettes and tobacco were safely secured in his backpack. Piper shoved a jar of onions under his nose, an offer which James politely declined.

"It's like a Boy Scout jamboree out there," Piper remarked absently.

James pulled out the photo of Mary and smiled as he remembered one of her anecdotes.

"I was in the Girl Guides you know," she had told him one summer evening, "it was such fun going on those camping trips all across the countryside. I remember one time, there was a group of Scouts over on the other side of the field and we kept pulling their tent pegs out of the ground. When they saw us, we ran away through the stinging nettles in our long skirts and they tried to chase after us in their shorts!" she said, laughing at the memory.

"I suppose it was like a kind of flirting and afterwards they invited us to their campfire where we sang songs and shared mugs of hot cocoa and biscuits with them. The next night we did the same thing again only they didn't bother chasing us, they just invited us over. I had my first ever kiss on that camp."

That last revelation had sent a small pang of insecure envy through James.

"No need to get jealous, my dear," she told him, spotting the tenseness in his face. "A little scout is no match for my big brave soldier."

The sound of a truck pulling up outside alerted them to the return of the two captains. Jones entered the building and disappeared upstairs whilst Spark walked round the back, leaving Smythe to his own devices.

"What did they say?" James asked him.

Smythe shrugged. "Not much. We just warned the mayor that the Germans are coming back and that everyone would be safer if they stayed in their houses."

"Any idea when?"

"Nah. Sometime in the next day or two is all Spark knows at the moment."

Spark entered the building a minute later, calling everyone outside. "Come on chaps, we've got some work to do. Need you all round the back as quick as you can."

When they got there, they were organised into groups and over the course of the next few hours they set about digging the beginnings of a series of defensive slit trenches and tank traps. The first few times that James thrust the edge of his spade into the earth he wondered what Nazi-created horrors he might be uncovering, but it wasn't long before his forehead was glistening with sweat and he lost himself in the work. Truckloads of men and armoured vehicles started turning up, initially in dribs and drabs, until it seemed like there was an endless stream of vehicles bringing supplies, engineers, and soldiers flooding into the area. Much to everyone's annoyance the tank drivers seemed to be doing nothing but get in the way and churn the ground up.

When James stopped for a rest he noticed that neither David, Piper, nor Smythe were anywhere to be seen. After realising that he was the only one who hadn't taken the opportunity to skive off doing some work James decided to take a look around and see what else was going on. He walked past officers studying maps, radio operators listening intently into their headphones as they twiddled and flicked half a dozen knobs and switches, and watched as porters shunted boxes of armaments around. One stack of crates in particular piqued his curiosity when he realised it was full of PIATs, the British equivalent of the American bazooka. James had always had something of a love-hate relationship with these odd-looking contraptions; they resembled a giant syringe and could be awkward to reload if you weren't tall enough to handle them properly. It required standing the shoulder-mounted device on the ground, stepping onto the shoulder rest, and then performing an odd combination of twisting, pulling, and lifting in order to get the spring to click back into place. To top it all off the recoil had a tendency to leave nasty bruises or maybe even a dislocated shoulder if you were particularly unlucky.

It was impossible for all the noise and activity to go unnoticed by the local residents and crowds of curious civilians watched all the digging and unloading with keen fascination. James felt an odd pang of jealousy when, off in the distance, he spotted a pretty blonde girl talking and laughing with some soldiers. As the evening wore on and the sky became ever darker, the chaotic sounds of an army hurriedly organising itself gradually quietened down and the civilians retreated back to their homes for dinner. Ration packs were distributed out, leaving James to make do with dried biscuits and tins of cold beef and pork, a marked change from the delights and treats that he had been feasting on over the past few days.

"Reckon Jerry will attack tonight?" someone asked as they took up their positions along the line.

James sniffed theatrically at the air. "Nah, the wind smells wrong and Jerry is a superstitious beast."

"If you say so, mate."

Truth be told, James didn't really want to discuss the likelihood of a German attack that night, especially with someone he didn't know. If the Germans were going to advance on them then they would do so and speculating about it did nothing but heighten the anticipation. The sound of someone belching loudly emanated from out of the darkness and James sniggered when, a few seconds later, a

168

disgusted voice called out "Can anyone else smell stale onions?"

As he stared up at the moon James found himself feeling comforted in the knowledge that no matter what happens, some things never changed.

***

Chapter Eight

The next morning James was disturbed by someone jumping down into the trench beside him. He blinked himself awake to see that David had materialised from nowhere.

"Morning," David greeted him.

"Yeah, it is," James acknowledged with a grunt. "Where've you been?"

"Having breakfast," David replied with a grin. "No point sleeping in a ditch when you can share a bed with someone warm and soft." He seemed to revel in the envious stares from those around him.

"Oh, yeah?" James asked with a grin, "What was his name?"

David ignored the jibe. "I even had myself a nice relaxing bath and a shave as well."

James looked at his own hands and saw that the creases were caked with grime and mud, with what seemed like an entire French garden hiding under his fingernails. This was in stark contrast to David who seemed to glow as if he were luminous.

"You got a spare fag?" David asked, his voice full of boyish optimism.

James rolled his eyes, acknowledging for the second time that some things never change and retrieved two white sticks from his pocket. "Only if you promise to be a good boy."

"Whatever you say, boss," David agreed.

The rest of the morning was taken up with strengthening the defences, moving supplies and equipment, along with trying to second guess what the officers were talking about as they huddled

170

together and passed decoded radio messages to each other. Just before lunchtime Captain Spark appeared and told his section of the line to take up their positions.

"Okay, chaps," he said, clasping his hands together, "Jerry is going to be popping along in an hour or two and I'm sad to report that it isn't a social visit he's blessing us with. He's going to be bringing tanks, guns, and lots of bad language with him, so make sure your mother is tucked up in bed before he gets here." He considered something for a moment before continuing. "No, scratch that, my mother is the scariest person I've ever met and has a deadly aim with her handbag. I suggest we round up all the coffin dodgers and slip some bricks into their purses when no-one's looking."

Snickers and sniggers could be heard from all along the line, much to Spark's visible delight. James found himself wondering how many theatres Spark could sell out if he ever decided to change career once the war was over.

"Anyway, Jerry is loading himself into his Panzers as we speak and we're the chaps who'll be putting a stop to it all. No need to worry though, as the only thing you'll find inside a Panzer is a pansy and that," Spark's face suddenly turned serious as he brought his hands up to his chest and clenched them into tight fists. "*That* is why we're going to reach inside his iron casks of shit and squeeze him until his balls are nothing but flaps of flesh. We'll take everything he has and make him beg for fucking mercy; we'll make him sorry he ever stepped outside his house and we'll make him pay for every torpedo that sank one of our ships; we'll make him pay for all the times our wives and girlfriends had to queue for hours for a loaf of bread; we'll make him regret every single bomb his planes dropped on our homes and once we're done we'll smash his face into the ground until he stops moving."

Spark paused for effect and let the silence do its work before spreading out his hands and calmly but firmly asking "Do I make myself clear?"

James, along with everyone around him, nodded and voiced their agreement with a heartfelt "Yes, Sir!" when Spark's face suddenly turned fierce as he roared at the top of his voice.

"Do I make myself clear?!?"

This simple, repeated question had the effect of condensing all of James' frustration, anger, and fear into a single pinpoint, one that plunged itself deep into an animalistic instinct he barely even knew existed and his mouth was roaring loudly and violently before his conscious mind knew what was happening.

Yes, Sir!

All along the line soldiers and officers from all walks of life, from all kinds of backgrounds and social standings roared, shouted, and bellowed in unison as if nothing else on earth mattered. Spark looked up and down the trench, nodding in satisfaction as if he was addressing each solider individually. When the noise died down he disappeared into the crowd.

Approximately an hour later the wind carried the seeds of a new sound to those with the keenest ears, one that made the hairs on the backs of their necks stand up. A gradual hush descended on the world as machines of war clanked and ground their way across the plains of France, filling James with nervous anticipation as the trench echoed with the clicks of men checking and rechecking their rifles one final time. He swallowed hard as the tops of trees and bushes began to wobble and sway as if the monsters of his childhood nightmares had finally come to life.

"Wait until they get close!" someone yelled, "Make every bullet count!"

Off in the distance a tank appeared, followed by a second and then a third, when suddenly the world was filled with a writhing mass of German soldiers and armoured vehicles of every type. Below the mechanical din a new sound could be heard, one that was harsh, guttural and alien, one that James quickly identified as belonging to German officers barking out orders to their men. He glanced down at his rifle and wondered how on earth it was going to be of any use against such an unstoppable military force. As the armada made its way towards him, James spotted a German head pop up from the top of a tank and shout something down at the soldiers below him. James ground his teeth in frustration as he realised it was a target well out of range of his own weapon when there was a sudden loud crack to his right. Looking down the trench line he caught sight of Piper pulling back the bolt lever on his sniper rifle, before turning back around just in time to see the tank commander disappearing under the tracks of his own war machine.

"Fucking outstanding shot there, chap!" called out a familiar voice.

James found himself filled with the kind of wonder and admiration usually reserved for a golfer who manages to swing a hole-in-one, yet Piper's face was utterly devoid of any signs of joy or victory, giving him the aura of a paranoid film star who despises all the adoration bestowed upon him. A burst of automatic gunfire went off first to James' left and then another to his right, when suddenly the entire world was thrown into a bewildering chaos as a dozen German soldiers collapsed inexplicably to the ground. There was a flash of light as a tank fired at the British line, sending a gigantic mound of earth up into the air as men, metal, and mud were obliterated and smashed into nothing. For the briefest of moments James was vaguely aware of movement in front of him, something that was large, deadly, and zipping through the air at an incredibly high speed, when a Panzer tank transformed from being a mighty cask of impenetrable military might into an exploding fireball. Men screamed as thick lumps of molten armour sliced through their flesh and waves of burning diesel erased them from existence.

A young soldier next to James hoisted a PIAT up onto his shoulder and took aim at an armoured vehicle that was charging towards them. As he pulled the trigger his body jerked and there was a metallic screech as the spring catapulted the PIAT round towards its target, whereupon it bounced uselessly off the side with a loud *clang!* James and the soldier looked at each other in dismay as they wondered if someone had swapped their ammunition for tins of beans.

"Reload it!" James bellowed, breaking the teenager out of his paralysis.

The soldier grabbed another round from the crate behind him and fumbled around as he struggled to get the awkward contraption ready for a second try. James snatched it from him, stood the PIAT on the ground, and twisted it around to snap the spring back into place.

"Ready!" James bellowed after swinging it up onto his shoulder.

A clammy hand appeared and loaded the round into the front of the weapon, before disappearing again. Another clammy hand gripped James' arm just as a voice that was still going through the final stages of puberty screamed at him to fire. James took aim and fired the weapon, sending the explosive charge hurtling through the air, grunting as the PIAT kicked hard against him. For a split second he thought he had missed but it clipped the rear of the tank, exploding and dislodging the tank track to bring it to a squealing, juddering halt.

"We got him!" the young soldier screamed, his face flush with a look of victory and euphoria that suggested he had just witnessed the final action of the war.

"Get your bloody head down!" James shouted, yanking him back to safety.

Although the tank had been crippled it hadn't been disarmed, something that the men inside it were all too aware of. The gun jerked into life and rotated around like an automaton, one that was determined to end humanity, one that wouldn't stop to obtain vengeance against any mortal that dared to attack it.

There was a flash and James was vaguely aware of something large passing a few inches above his head when a huge explosion from behind caused him to hurl himself to the floor. A wave of hot air washed down into the trench, filling James' nose, mouth, and throat with the stench of burning diesel as his ears rang with the screams of men being burnt alive. As James stood back up again he grabbed his rifle and started firing at groups of German soldiers, relishing every scream and every stumble as he pulled his trigger again and again. The entire battlefield seemed to be warping and changing like a cloud in a thunderstorm, and James found it hard to focus on the advancing infantry as they shifted about like swarms of locusts. The automatic machine guns tore gaping holes in their lines only for them to close up again like a wound that could heal itself in the blink of an eye. Tanks and mobile gun batteries charged around as they battled to outflank and outmanoeuvre each other in a never-ending game of chess. As James continued firing round after round at the advancing German hordes, someone shoved their way past him.

"These bastards are overrunning us here, we need to fall back and regroup!" Spark yelled at the top of his voice.

When James looked across the battlefield, it once again seemed to have changed from what it was only a few moments ago as pulverised tanks and armoured vehicles burned like vanquished demons belching thick columns of poisonous black smoke up into the sky. The dead lay torn and twisted like a collection of battered and discarded children's dolls whilst the dying clutched at their own intestines and screamed for their mothers.

"Come on! We've got to fall back!" Spark roared, his face turning red as the veins in his neck bulged beneath the skin.

James followed Spark along the trench, stepping and stumbling over dead men and shorn limbs as he went. A soldier's hand inexplicably turned red and useless as a stray bit of shrapnel sheared off his thumb and the *ding!* and *ting!* of bullets ricocheting off helmets was alarming and unsettling. A German tank suddenly roared up to the top of their defensive wall, pausing at the top like a rocking horse at the limit of its backward tilt, before plunging down the other side and jamming itself into the trap. Within seconds British soldiers were gleefully clambering over it like a colony of ants attacking a giant beetle that had wandered into their lair. The fastest climber yanked open the hatch and fired his gun at the men inside as two others grabbed hand grenades from their belts and fought to be the first one to shove an explosive into the hole. Seconds later two muffled explosions went off and a dark red mist sprayed out through the slit at the front. It was only when the first soldier opened the hatch up again and bellowed foreign obscenities at anyone who might still be down there that he realised it was Smythe. James continued following the men in front of him until they emerged at a point not too far from the building that had served as his home for the last few days.

"This way, chaps!" yelled Spark from somewhere up ahead.

They ran down an alley and emerged out onto on a road that James didn't recognise. Down to his left a German tank was lying in wait for them and everyone scrambled to retreat back the way they had just come. There was a loud *boom!* and James watched as the side of a building cracked open, collapsing in on itself like a dollhouse that had been hit by a sledgehammer. A tall chimney stack that ran up the side of the building tottered like an ancient oak tree that had finally succumbed to the woodsman's axe before tumbling into the road and crushing anyone who had been standing in its shadow. James darted down another alley and as he emerged onto another road, three British tanks roared past and almost squashed him beneath their tracks. He spotted a familiar figure kicking down the door of what looked to be an old warehouse.

"David? What you doing?" he asked.

When David turned around there was a peculiar expression on his face, one that could have been surprise but was more likely to be annoyance. "Thought this building would give us a good vantage point," he explained with a shrug.

Somewhere in the back of James' mind the suspicion that David was lying briefly took hold. Two more soldiers appeared behind them and James gestured to the one with a machine gun.

"Put some lead into that lock, it's the only way we'll get the bloody thing open."

The soldier nodded and emptied an entire clip into the door, which finally relented after David gave it several more swift kicks. A set of stairs lay just inside the building and as they ran towards them, more soldiers filtered in behind them.

"If we go over to the other side on the top floor, we'll be able to see the Germans as they try to make their way through the town," James yelled out.

They clumped their way to the next floor and went through a door that led them into a large open area that stretched out across the length of the building. James walked over to a window and smashed the glass out with his rifle, and within a few seconds the room was filled with the sound of heavy boots and windows breaking as the other soldiers set themselves up into defensive positions. James surveyed the view they had, quickly taking a mental note of all the corners and entry points whilst David dragged over a crate and lit himself a cigarette. Outside they heard the muffled roar of a diesel engine as an unseen tank raced past the building. James looked at David and held his gaze for a few moments before giving him a small reassuring nod. David nodded back, took the cigarette from his mouth, and let out a long stream of smoke.

"That French tobacco any good?" James enquired conversationally.

A smile appeared on David's face, one that took James by surprise because it looked completely genuine. "Try it," he said, handing the cigarette over.

James took it from him and placed it between his lips. As a non-smoker it was something that felt alien and uncomfortable and his head buzzed furiously as the nicotine tickled at the edges of his consciousness. He coughed as his lungs filled with what could only be smoke from a bonfire.

"Yeah, thanks," James just about managed to say, handing the cigarette back.

David laughed. "Strong stuff, eh? Puts hairs on your bollocks that's for sure."

A noise from outside brought James' senses back to normal and he caught sight of a German soldier popping his head around the corner of a building.

"They're here!" he yelled, firing off a few shots from his rifle. The sound of gunfire echoed loudly around the room as everyone followed his cue and where the German soldier's head had been only moments before, the air was suddenly alive with dust and bits of masonry as bullets ricocheted off the brickwork.

"Bottom right!" James bellowed as three figures in grey ran out from behind a wall. Just as they got halfway across the road, they flopped inexplicably to the ground as a dozen rounds thundered into them, their bodies jerking as vengeful foes made sure they were truly dead.

There was a loud commotion from outside as German officers shouted and bellowed instructions at each other from behind cover. The remains of the windows shattered as the Germans returned fire from a position that James was unable to see and he looked to his left just in time to see a fellow soldier jerk backwards and fall to the floor. There was another roar of a diesel engine and James caught sight of a flash of grey as an armoured vehicle shot past the gap between two buildings. Chaos and confusion returned as the aggressive German shouts suddenly turned into a panic-stricken screaming as a loud *boom!* and a huge explosion caused James to instinctively duck his head down. It was only when he saw the columns of thick black smoke rising into the air from behind a house that he even knew where it had happened. More German soldiers appeared and the windows of James' building came alive as the defenders unleashed a murderous hail of bullets, covering the road with the blood of the dead and the screams of the dying. The clanking squeal of caterpillar tracks announced the arrival of more tanks, though James had no idea which side they belonged to. Through the branches of a tree he saw the sparkling display of bullets bouncing and ricocheting uselessly off thick plates of impenetrable armour. There was another loud *boom!* and James and David exchanged a nervous glance as the entire building shook beneath them. A new sound reached their ears, one of heavy boots on stairs, reminding them of the relentless nature of the German war machine.

"They're right here inside the building!" James screamed.

The noise became louder and James felt a cold chill run through him when he heard what could only be German voices on the other side of the door. A set of holes suddenly appeared in the wall as something small and deadly zipped past James' ear, followed by a heavy thump as someone behind him collapsed to the floor, the front of their uniform darkening as blood gushed from a wound in his stomach. The building shook again, causing David to curse as he cut his hand trying to fix a bayonet onto his rifle. The door flew open, revealing a German soldier who managed to take no more than one step into the room before being cut down in a hail of gunfire. James staggered and went down on knee as the ground shifted beneath his feet and large cracks zig-zagged across the wooden floorboards. He looked up just in time to see David thrusting the point of his bayonet deep into a German soldier's chest. As he tried to stand back up the floor felt soft and bouncy like he was standing on a pillow and James felt himself falling backwards as if a rug were being pulled out from underneath him. He caught sight of David leaping towards the doorway before finding himself consumed with the sensation of weightlessness as debris, dust, and chunks of wood swirled all around him. As he fell through the air James could only watch in abject confusion as his feet, his rifle, and the ceiling seemed to be floating away from him. Something slammed into the back of his head, something that sent an immense pain coursing through his entire body, when his rifle and everything else in the world came rushing back down towards him. Bright flashes dominated his vision as he struggled to stay focused on anything and a rising panic flowed through him as a tiny dot of light in the corner of his eye started swelling and expanding like an exploding star. He thought about Mary, of the way she walked barefoot in the garden just to leave her prints in the early morning dew, of the way she held a pen so lightly it was a wonder that she could even write, of the way she could let out a sigh that said a thousand words. He thought of everything, he thought of nothing, and all of it overwhelmed his fragile hold on consciousness in an instant.

***

Chapter Nine

His head hurt and he couldn't move his arms...
nor anything else for that matter. Although he was
unable to open his eyes, somehow he knew, he just
knew, that he had been locked up in a secret room that
all the circus freaks were shoved into when the show
finally leaves town. Someone had done something
terrible and unnatural and now his head had swollen
to three times its normal size, and instead of putting
him out of his misery the doctors had strapped him to
a bed so they could stare at his immense cranium,
prodding it with needles and instruments and writing
meaningless bits of nonsense on their clipboards.

"Hang on," said a voice, "we've got signs of life
at last."

James mustered up all his strength and tried to
move his enormous head, which had now swollen to
ten times its normal size, barely able to hold back the
tears of grief. An immense pain wracked his entire
body and he knew, he just *knew,* that his frail neck
was snapping under the immense strain. A quick and
merciful death would be a relief for everyone.

"Hmmm, maybe not," lamented the voice.

James brought himself back under control,
determined to let his last few moments be serene and
peaceful. Random colours started to slowly seep
through the dark grey veil in front of him and there
was a familiar noise that reminded him of sparks,
flames, and French tobacco. He turned his head
towards the sound and the random colours gradually
dissolved into shapes that he recognised and loved.

"David?" James croaked.

"The very one," David replied, sitting up straight in his chair and taking his feet down from James' bed. "How'd you feel?"

"Dunno," James replied, feeling stupid, "head hurts."

"Yeah, you've been out for a couple of days."

This revelation sent a bolt of surprise through him, almost like he was being told that he had overslept and missed his own wedding. His indignant mind reacted by demanding that he sit up and ask for an explanation, but his body didn't seem to care and did little more than twitch the bed sheets.

"They've been injecting you with all sorts, mate," David told him, holding back a grin, "and you've asked three different nurses to marry you."

James grunted out a small laugh and blinked as he wondered why his arms had been replaced with white coils of fabric. His fingers twitched pathetically, steadfastly refusing his demands for them to scratch at the maddening itching sensation that was now darting and racing across every inch of his skin.

"You took a hell of a fall," continued David, "thought you were done for. One moment you were shouting your head off and the next thing I know you'd vanished. You're pretty tough for a pretty boy." There was a note of relief in his voice.

James struggled to remember anything of note. "What happened?"

David shrugged. "A tank tried to take out the building we were in and most of the floor collapsed underneath us. I just about managed to jump out the way and was left stranded in the doorway. Them

Germans were storming up the stairs but couldn't see me, I almost ran out of ammunition shooting the silly buggers."

James was silent for a moment. "Did we win?" he asked. For some reason the answer to this question was of the utmost importance, a matter of pride above all else.

"Yeah," David answered without much conviction, "though the town is in a right mess and I don't think we'll be getting any free pastries for a while."

James blinked as his confused and distressed mind danced between elation and despair.

"The coffee shop," David patiently explained. "It's not there anymore."

His memory of the coffee shop rose up from beneath the blanket of fog that was clouding his mind, sticking out and holding his attention like a broken bone poking out from a disfigured arm. He closed his eyes and waited as more images began emerging from the woollen recesses of his subconscious, filling him with a mixture of emotions.

"What about…" he asked, struggling to decide which question to ask first, "what about Piper?"

David let out a small laugh and shook his head. "Yeah, he made it. Not so much as a scratch or a bead of sweat on him when the battle was over. Then he went and nearly got himself killed rescuing some kids that were trapped under a collapsed house. Daft sod."

James smiled, grateful to hear what he considered to be good news. "And Smythe?"

David glanced down at the floor for a moment, leaving James to assume the worst. "Yeah, he's okay, but he looks about ten years older. Spark had him interrogating the prisoners until we realised that he was just telling them Germany is a place of evil."

James raised his eyebrows in surprise. "That's…" he began, letting the sentence trail off. "Actually, I think I know how he feels."

"Yeah, I thought you might," David replied somewhat cryptically. "He'll be alright in a couple of days after he's had a bacon sandwich and a shower."

The thought of home comforts sent an image of blonde hair shooting out from the fog that was still at the back of James' mind. "What about the girls?"

David's face went blank as he tried to remember who he was talking about. "Oh, them. No idea, not seen them." He noted the look of sadness on James' face before continuing, "Some of the smarter civilians moved to the other side of town just before the Germans first attacked. They were pretty smart, right?"

"Yeah," James replied quickly, although his answer was more hopeful than realistic. As he recalled Angelette's face, the attributes that came to mind were scared and vulnerable rather than smart and worldly. Not to mention the fact that she had a disabled father to worry about as well. And what if he was the type of stubborn ex-soldier who preferred to stay and fight rather than flee from his home? "Yeah, I'm sure they're fine."

A young soldier on crutches hobbled awkwardly through the hospital ward and James' mind once again itched beneath the fog. "There was some kid with me in the trench," he said, grasping for the details. "He was struggling with one of those anti-tank guns. I wonder what happened to him."

David puffed out his cheeks. "You've just described half the army, mate. Any idea what his name was?"

James opened his mouth and shut it again. "No," he confessed, "no idea at all."

The two of them looked at each other for a moment. "Oh, almost forgot," said David, reaching into one his pockets. "I got you a present I thought you'd like."

James was reminded that his body was still healing as David's arm disappeared into a blur of quick movement, when something heavy landed in his lap, something that was black and familiar, something that triggered memories both good and bad.

It was a German Luger pistol.

James grunted as he reached for it, beads of sweat breaking out on his forehead as he forced his fingers to close around the handgrip of the weapon in front of him.

"Steady on, I think it's still loaded," David remarked, theatrically leaning backwards in his chair.

James barely heard him and slowly turned the Luger around in his hands, relishing the quality of workmanship that seemed to emanate from so many of the weapons that the German war factories churned out. The smell of gun grease triggered another memory that had been hiding away from him, one that caused a big smile to spread across his face.

"She's right," he said, nodding to himself, "she's *always* right."

"Who?" enquired David.

"The enemy isn't so frightening when you've dismantled his weapons and placed all the bits next to a vase of flowers."

David frowned. "You feeling alright? Want me to get the nurse for you?"

James laughed, ignoring the pain that was flaring and racing up his chest. "Nah, I'm fine." He leaned back against his pillow and closed his eyes as a wave of fresh tiredness washed over him.

"I'm absolutely fine."

***

Thank you for reading!
Reviews are the lifeblood of independent authors such as myself. Please consider leaving a short review on the site that you bought this book from.

Email - mcargill79@gmail.com
Twitter - @MichaelCargill1
Website of satire -
http://michaelcargill.wordpress.com/
http://www.facebook.com/MichaelCargillAuthor

Excerpts from my website:

Everyone should brush, floss, and barf thrice daily

Hi there! My name is David Wrongford and I'm here to tell you all about my innovative new dental routine.

Dental hygiene is important not only for dentists but also for the general wellbeing of society as a whole. I'll explain my point via the use of an analogy about food: if you bought an apple, you wouldn't set it down next to another apple that had turned rotten; instead, you'd finish it off before your greedy neighbour noticed it.

See? Makes perfect sense. Food analogies are good because food is tasty and most people will have consumed at least one bit of food at some point in their lives.

My dental routine starts off with three minutes of vigorous brushing, a process that practically guarantees drawing some blood from the stubborn bastards that are my gums. As the saying goes: old enough to bleed, yes indeed. Following on from that, whilst my gums are still screaming furiously at me, I give them a good kicking with the flossing cord – and by Jove do they kick up a stink! I did ask my dentist if there's such a thing as barbed flossing wire but he said he didn't know of any.

Finally, and this is my favourite part, we come to the pisté tea resistancé: the barfing. I select two fingers from my right hand, press the tips of them against the back of my throat, and let the magic of nature do the rest. Out come all those nasty bits of offal from the night before and all of a sudden my head will be spinning with delight and happiness. Don't be shy or nervous about it, just let it all out. You ever seen a cow do a doo-doo? It just expels it's nonsense as quick as a flash and carries right on with its business as if nothing happened. In fact cats are a bit like that as well and everyone loves cats.

If you find that a chunk of sweetcorn or a sliver of a noodle gets stuck in between your teeth, don't worry: I like to leave it there as a final 'up yours' to my gums.

Lastly, be sure to 'go naked' with your fingers during the barfing stage; I did experiment with some protective sheaths a while ago but found that the rubber kills the sensation somewhat.

**

Hulk Hogan reviews a tin of Heinz baked beans

As some of ya'll already know, I've been struggling to make ends meet since I retired from the ring as no-one's willing to sponsor me no more. Turns out that demand for a large fella who can suffocate small children in between his thighs is dwindling; I've had rejection letters from just about everyone, including Nike, Adidas, and even them people who make that Vaseline stuff. That last one hurt real bad seeing as how much of it I've used over the years.

Things are so bad that I've had to resort to buying tinned foods just to keep my energy levels up, which brings me onto today's breakfast – baked beans.

Now I've never been much of a reader but the instructions on how to open this gosh-darn tin are mighty hard to read, so mayhaps one of y'all can gimme a hand? Oh, silly me, I had it all upside down! And now looky, there's one of them ringy pull things staring right up at me. Why'd they have to hide it away like that, folks get all confused with such trickery.

Okay, now that the lid's off I can see some little cocoon things swimming around in some kind of red goo. Now, I guess that thems are the beans but they're far too small for me to get hold of so I'll have to use a cocktail stick to jab 'em before they start hatching. Hmmm, they taste kinda squishy; kinda nice; but also kinda cold and, if I'm honest, I prefer a hot breakfast to a cold one. Let me just pour them into my pants for a minute, there's plenty of warm down there.

Gosh darn it, the goo is starting to seep through the spandex! Gimme a sec while I scoop it all back out and finish it off in one go. Okay, well, this time it was much warmer but there were several crunchy little hairs mixed up with the sauce. I'm not sure where they came from but it was like eating raw spaghetti… and boy, do I like my spaghetti!

Well, it has to be said, these baked beans ain't half bad. I think I might give the barbecue frankfurters a try next week.

***

38436993R00118

Made in the USA
Charleston, SC
06 February 2015